Furiousfotog

BROKEN DEEDS MC

SECOND GENERATION #4

By Esther E. Schmidt

Cover design by:

Esther E. Schmidt

Editor #1:

Christi Durbin

Editor #2:

Virginia Tesi Carey

Cover model:

Wesley Dutchman

Photographer:

Golden Czermak, FuriousFotog

DEDICATION

To friendship.

It comes in many ways and its depth
is valued by many, though tested by some.
Stay true to yourself and honor a bond
that's equal and soul deep.

CHAPTER ONE

JERSEY

"Let me get this straight." Archer crosses his inked arms in front of his chest and narrows his eyes. "You're telling me Baton could be alive?"

I wince slightly and point at my laptop. "Check the data. When Baton was badly injured and Benedict was flying them back after the mission, Baton asked him to turn off the trackers they had inside of them. You can see the time and location the signal died, right above the sea where Baton let himself fall out of the helicopter. But when you deactivate these trackers, they have a twelve-hour window where they store data. A precaution in case someone gets kidnapped and the kidnappers turn it off. Well, in this case it shows us where Baton's body went. And I'm telling you, he might have jumped out of that helicopter Benedict was flying, but I don't think he dove into the sea to die. Not right away for that matter."

Archer falls back into his chair and mutters, "Dead men don't go from a clinic to a hotel room."

"Right." I release a deep sigh and silence fills the room.

Baton and Benedict are twins. Sons of North and Reva and are both members of Broken Deeds MC. Our MC handles cases the government can't close. They are allowed to use any means necessary and all of this entails high-risk missions, cold cases, investigations, all parts can be a matter of life and death.

In this case one of the twins was badly injured and both thought he wasn't going to make it. Baton being Baton–and the insane statement he used to say ever since he was a kid–wanted to live forever. I grew up with all the other kids of the first generation since I am one too. And I know Baton, he has always been an "all in, all out," person. And to make it possible not to die, he asked Benedict to turn off their tracker so he could hurl himself into the sea and make Benedict take his name and place in life.

Insanely stupid and selfish if you ask me. And no one knew about the loss of Baton and the switch Benedict made; no one except for Benedict himself who pretended to be Baton. And no one thought anything of it as he showed everyone a video where "Benedict" blabbered about needing to go away for a while and live his life apart from Broken Deeds MC for the time being.

No one heard from him again so it was just Baton. Well, Benedict. Yeah, confusing for sure and I can't start to comprehend how it must have been for Benedict to live his life as his brother, facing his family and everyone else of the MC on a daily basis.

That is until Baton, or who we thought was Baton, got hurt and was taken by the cartel. His old lady asked me if I could turn both trackers back on. No one has ever turned a tracker back on but I tried and it worked. It's then I noticed the irregular data of one of the trackers but I couldn't check into it because we had to find Benedict. We were able to find and save him, but now we have to deal with the information I discovered.

"And no one knows about this?" Archer rubs a hand over his mouth and I can see the pain sliding over his face.

It's a lot to take in. More for Archer because he's the president of this MC. Not only is he responsible for all his brothers but this also involves a family matter; Baton and Benedict being the children of North, a biker of the first generation.

All of us have grown up together. I might be a woman, but I grew up in this MC. My father is still a full member and works on active cases and I sometimes help out whenever I can. I'm good with computers. I hate it but it's been useful.

My mother runs her own business which designs, produces, and sells stuffed animals. I'm doing that too, well…not the stuffed animals part, my creations are a bit different. I create twisted dolls and enjoy creating and designing a lot more than computer stuff. Only my parents know about my special designs and support me. I do have to say, over the years it has brought me a pretty steady income.

My ex-boyfriend called me a nutjob when I finally told him about what I did for a living. I could say he was the nutjob but I really don't want to be thinking of him or the time we spent together. Besides, he's no longer among the living because the cheating bastard ran across the road to get to the bitch he cheated on me with and got hit by a truck. Talk about irony. I was still cursing his cheating ass while coming down the porch.

"Well?" Archer snaps.

Well, what? Oh, right. "No, no one knows about it. I kept it to myself and dove into the data when I had the time. I mean, we all had Benedict and the cartel to focus on and worry about and Baton's death, missing body, whatever. Well, it has been months since it happened. We only recently found out about the switch and the loss of Baton when Benedict finally shared his burden. And I would like to be the one who is going to look into it. First thing I'll do is travel to the clinic. I'll hack into their system to see if there is any data stored. Then I'll ask around, then check out the hotel where the tracker left the final location, and–"

"Whoa there. I was thinking it would make more sense to put Austin on it and–"

"Austin? No. Just…no. I understand he has the experience and resources but this needs to be done by one of us." *Not to mention Austin is an insensitive asshole*, I mentally add.

"Shut those rambling lips, Jersey. What I was going to say when you cut me off was that I'm going to put Austin on it and have you work with him because I do agree, this needs to be supervised by one of us. I can't leave to track down leads right now and to be honest? This is too delicate to let one of my brothers handle it. I'm only going to tell my wife and she's also your backup. Bee will be there if you have questions or need another brain for computer stuff. Anything else, you report directly to me."

Shock and surprise fill me. I honestly didn't think he would give me a chance.

"Don't look so surprised, Jersey," Archer says and he grabs his phone, it seems he's texting someone. "You might not be wearing a leather cut, or have the old lady status, but you are a part of Broken Deeds MC. You've proven your talents many times over when we asked for your help. With you moving back here, and if you're interested, I'd like to use your expertise on a regular basis."

"I'm interested," I squeak.

Archer shoots me a grin. "Good. Give it all you got and we'll go from there. Go, pack a bag and don't tell anyone. I just texted Austin to do the same and meet me at the diner across town. I'm going to drop you off so you can fill him in."

Drop me... "He's not going to like it if I'm the one telling him what to do."

The annoying man simply shrugs and his eyes slide to the phone when it lights up with a text message. "I'm the president of this MC. He might be from a different one but I hire him on a regular basis and he's never complained about anyone who debriefed him about an assignment. Besides, I have his reply right here agreeing with the assignment. The both of you report to me but have to work together. And if he so much as touches one hair on your head or hurts you, you contact me at once, understood?"

He's already hurt me by stating I'm a useless person, my mind offers. I remember all too vividly how he dismissed me when I found crucial information in the cartel case.

"Your work is done. We can handle it from here and I'm sure we could have handled it without your help. Others have the same qualities as you and some might even–" That's where I cut off his ramblings. I heard enough. Hell, it's what has been screaming through my head because it was the exact same thing my cheating boyfriend said right before he died.

You're nothing special. Mediocre at best. I should have never stuck my dick inside you because you and your twisted mind are too dirty to so much as finger-fuck with a stick.

I shut my rambling mind off and focus on Archer. "You got it."

He gives me a tight nod. "Be ready in ten minutes. I'll be waiting out front. And tell your nosy father I put you on a case. If he gives you shit, send him to me, I'll handle it."

I close my laptop and dash out. Heading through the back of the clubhouse I walk the short distance to my parents' house. I've been staying with them ever since the whole incident with my ex. I was living out of state and I just put my condo up for sale because with all the bad memories of my ex and having him dying in the street I wanted a clean break and to move back to my hometown.

Walking inside I notice both my mother and father are in the kitchen.

"Hey," I quip and walk backwards toward the stairs. "I'm heading out for a few days. Archer asked me to work a case, computer stuff. If you have any questions just ask him. I have to pack a bag. I'm leaving in ten minutes."

"He did?" my father rumbles.

I freeze in my tracks. He's always been overprotective and wants to know my every move. He didn't like it when I moved out of state but understood and respected my choices. Except, with everything that happened with my ex dying in front of me…the overprotective element has returned full force.

I expect for him to shoot a firing squad of questions at me but he just simply says, "Well, move your ass and get to it."

Suspicion rears its ugly head and now I'm the one asking, "Why are you smiling?"

My mother pats his chest and gives me a warm look. "He's happy you're working. Accepting work here. If you accept a job from Archer, maybe you'll stay and not go back to your condo or buy something else in that state but move home instead."

My forehead furrows. "I'm not going back. I told you guys, I'm staying here. As soon as the condo is sold I'll head back to get the last of my stuff and then I'll start house hunting around here."

Dad points at his watch. "Better not keep Prez waiting."

"Shit," I grumble and head up the stairs to pack a bag.

I left my place in a hurry due to everything that happened with my ex. It's the reason most of my personal things are still there; not wanting the clinging memories of my life. It was more of a rebellious state of mind to move miles away from my family; feeling the need to make it on my own. All I've known growing up was the MC and the safe bubble that came with it.

Moving to another state gave me a clean cut and a chance to develop myself without the support and hovering alpha males trying to protect me from all sides. I've always been one to think failure and trying grants you valuable life lessons, and they mold you into the person you are today.

It's like designing a new doll from scratch and seeing what works or what absolutely doesn't. You find out soon enough during the process or find out the results once it's finished. Either way I've learned a lot and with the failure in my relationship with my ex. The cheating, the degrading and mental smackdown in the end is something I didn't see coming. One thing's for sure; I'm done with life lessons for now.

Hence the determination to sell my condo and move back permanently. My business is thriving and I can balance the new designs and getting them in production with enough time to also take cases like Archer offered. It's a balance I welcome and allows me to combine work and family.

I glance around my old bedroom and think of what else to put in my backpack besides two pair of jeans, two pairs of leggings, a few shirts, underwear and bras, my brush, and a toothbrush. My laptop is in there along with my notebook so I guess that's everything. Hell, it's practically everything I have here since I left everything behind when I left in a hurry.

Heading downstairs with two minutes to spare, I say goodbye to my parents and head back to the clubhouse where I find Archer out front in the parking lot beside his truck. When he sees me, he jumps into the front and starts the engine.

We're on our way to the diner when he says, "I can only drop you off because I just received an update about Benedict. He pulled through the night with a severe concussion. I also need to have a conversation about the Baton situation with Ellory. I'm going to let her know I've put you and Austin on the case since she's the one who put us on Baton's trail when she suggested to turn the tracker back on to find Benedict."

"Sound logical," I reply. "It's the closest thing to telling Benedict since I imagine he has to take it slow for the next week or so with his second severe concussion in what? Two weeks?"

"Right." Is all the reply he gives as he keeps his eyes on the road in front of him.

He parks in front of the diner and only gives me the words, "Call or text if you need anything or if there are any developments."

"Will do," I tell him and hop out of the truck.

I swing my backpack over my shoulder and close the door. Archer doesn't wait but drives off. I'm about to head into the diner to grab myself a choco-late milkshake but I hear a faint rumble and easily recognize the sound of a Harley approaching.

The bike itself is impressive, but the neanderthal

handling it is a man who has been the star of many erotic dreams. Yes, I admit, growing up I had a major crush on him. Maybe it was the whole unreachable element with Austin being from another MC, or the fact he's unlike any other person I've met.

He for sure isn't an easy man to be around. Growing up as a kid he wasn't either. Our MCs are connected through his family–Archer's mom, Lynn, is the old lady of the former president Deeds and her brother is the president of Areion Fury MC. Oh, and Archer married the daughter of the vice president of Areion Fury MC as well.

Needless to say, in the past it has led to some complications. Though, due to all connections, the two MCs have also forged a solid foundation. Hence the frequent barbeques, meetings, gatherings, events, and such growing up. The second generation of both MCs know one another, and where Broken Deeds MC had a shift in leadership, Areion Fury is still led by the first generation.

The irritation on Austin's face reminds me of the fact my crush on this man died a few days ago and was what it was; a childhood crush. He's just like any other man reminding me how they stomp on your self-esteem for no reason whatsoever.

Austin might excel in stomping on self-esteem since the man seems to lack any emotion and social skills and only thrives on facts and technicalities. He's rude and doesn't think twice to throw said facts and opinions at anyone standing in front of him. I mean, I appreciate honesty but with him it's always the raw data while others carefully pick their words to bring the message the easy, and most humane way.

Whatever, he's an asshole. And the way he's stomping my way with murder in his eyes reminds me about the last time he blurted out how others could manage without my help. Great. He's going to be a ray of sunshine when he hears Archer hired him to help me on a case.

"What are you doing here alone? What's in the backpack? Are you leaving?" he growls in a demanding tone.

Any other woman would be intimidated by the burly biker closing in. But I've grown up around neanderthals and this massive, bald, scruffy-jawed, overly inked muscled biker doesn't scare me. In fact, he pisses me off.

I close the distance between us with two strides and jab a finger against his naked chest. "None of your damn business, asshole. And who the hell only wears a leather cut and no shirt while riding a bike?"

His forehead furrows and those dark brown eyes fill with confusion. Probably wondering why I would throw out a question about his naked torso. But really, it's hard to concentrate seeing him with only a leather…what the hell?

"Sophia? Who is she and why do you have her name inked on your freaking forehead?" I gasp. "Did you claim an old lady in the last few days?"

Right above his left eyebrow is her name written with swirls. No one would ink a name on their skin unless it's a child or a lover or your mom, whatever. And Areion Fury doesn't have the same rule with inking a property patch when a biker takes an old lady.

"Loyalty, unconditional love, and understanding,"

the man supplies, adding to the mystery and not giving any details.

If my crush on this man was still flaming inside me, he would have stomped it into a smothering state where nothing would survive. I'm fairly sure since his statement clearly said Sophia is it for him.

Work, my brain screams at me to switch topics and focus on something else. I'm thankful not to lose my mind in this moment, it would be quite pathetic, really.

"Archer hired you for a case I'm working on. Let's go inside the diner, I want a milkshake and you need some details before we hit the road." I don't wait for a reply but spin around and speed walk toward the diner.

I grab my phone and shoot a text to Beatrice. She grew up in Areion Fury MC as the daughter of the vice president and still visits her parents regularly. If anyone would know who the heck Sophia is, it'll be her. Not that it matters, I'm just soothing my curiosity since I'm stuck with this asshole.

And at this point I don't even care if he follows

me into the diner or not. I knew it was a mistake to agree to work together. But at the same time, I refuse to let him stomp all over me. Working together means give and take, meaning this asshole needs to give a little because I'm not handing him shit and won't allow for any man to take something from me ever again.

CHAPTER TWO

AUSTIN

I mentally groan when I see Jersey's curvy ass sway away from me. And it's always walking a-fucking-way. Hell, every other woman runs away from me just as fast as they scurry toward me, but there's one difference.

I couldn't care less about those women. Jersey, though? It's complicated. Mainly because of who I am and how my brain works. Not to mention she's Broken Deeds MC and the fact she recently went through shit no woman should have to experience. A deep sigh rips from my throat and I stomp my way into the diner.

Jersey heads for a booth in the corner and I stride toward her and slip in across from her. A waitress instantly appears and sweetly asks me what I would like to order. I'm hungry since I missed breakfast and I have no clue how long we will be here or where we're going. And I do have a lead to squeeze in a little over an hour, concerning a case I'm working on.

I direct my attention to Jersey. "I'm hungry. Are we eating before we hit the road?"

She completely ignores me and gives the waitress a sweet smile. "I would like a chocolate milkshake and a burger, double pickles, please."

The waitress nods but not once does she give Jersey her eyes and it pisses me off. "Giving a customer your gaze makes them feel welcome. Only giving male customers fuck-me eyes won't give you any more tip money since the woman sitting across from me is buying. Needless to say, you're not my type so fucking is out of the question. And since I have your attention, I'd like two burgers, double fries, and a coffee."

The waitress' face is beet-red and it transitions

from shock to anger and is now shooting daggers at me before she rushes off like her apron is on fire. Like I said; women around me disappear faster than they appear.

"She's going to spit in your coffee, lick the bread of your burgers, and drop your fries on the floor before putting them back on your plate. You know that, right?"

I grimace and glance at the counter. "She's too lazy to go behind the counter so I think we're good."

"*We*'re good? It was you who not so gently told her not to give you 'fuck-me eyes' and how she's not doing her job and was rude all in one go. Oh, and let's not forget the 'Fucking is out of the question,' part. Real subtle."

All I can do is shrug. "It was the truth. I never beat around the bush and call it the way I see it."

"Right," she snaps and grabs her phone when it makes a sound.

She reads the message and sadness overtakes her face. Her caramel eyes with a swirl of dark brown mist up. She quickly shoves the phone back into her pocket and slides her silky looking brown hair behind her ear.

I'm about to ask her what's wrong but she knocks the wind out of me when she says, "I'm sorry about your girl, Sophia."

I only give a grunt, not wanting to dwell on it too much, but I should have known she wouldn't let it go. Jersey is the only damn one who always gets in my face no matter what I say. The woman never backs off and completely dismisses my personal space. But I have to confess, it's actually something I like about her. Though, I'll never openly confess to it.

She's always overly sweet, teasing, and a positive force to be reckoned with. Except for the confrontation we had in church of Broken Deeds MC a few days ago. It happened because nobody fucking told me about what happened to her. How was I supposed to know her ex cheated on her and died before her eyes?

I was my usual asshole-self and might have been agitated enough to take it out on her and in the end, I said shit I didn't mean. Something that must have triggered stuff she went through or was said by her asshole ex because she took a swing at me. I caught her wrist in time to prevent it, but still…she was right: I earned a punch to the face.

"I'm sorry for what I said in church," I grunt.

She tilts her head and her gaze slides over me, fucking tickling my skin where it lands until she blinks and asks, "How did she die?"

Fuck. I'd hoped to turn the conversation back to her instead of talking about my dog. I'm not one to have or show emotions due to the fact that my brain works differently. For one I inherited the photographic memory from my father, allowing me to take in every damn detail of my surroundings with a mere glance.

It's an overload of information I have to compartmentalize in order to stay sane because it comes with a thought process when I analyze people and everything else. Not to mention, I don't understand most emotions since they're a chemical reaction from your body. See? I'm simply not a people person and prefer the raw data because statistics I understand.

Secondly, due to this and the ability to suck up intelligence without much effort, my brain basically functions on statistics. Not fun if you calculate every damn move and every damn person and know through body language what the person's intentions are. And most times it's not good; people like to lie straight to your face. They hide their true intentions and hide behind a façade I can easily poke through.

Except for this woman sitting across from me. She's one of the rare people who can surprise me. Being able to rattle the first thing that comes to mind without any shame or either act completely out of place or not at all. Intriguing but frustrating at the same time because she's unpredictable and it makes me unhinged.

I glance at my inked hand and curl my fingers into a fist as I recite facts. "She was a retired service dog. I shouldn't have taken her with me during a stakeout. She caught a bullet meant for me. She died."

Her tiny hand covers mine triggering an electric current of awareness to jolt through my body. Fuck.

I felt the same thing when I wrapped my fingers around her wrist when she wanted to punch me a few days ago. And if a mere touch causes such a reaction, I can only imagine what it would feel like to bury my cock deep inside her pussy.

"Sorry to interrupt the moment. Here's your milkshake, miss." The waitress gives her full attention to Jersey and places my coffee on the table without giving me a word or a glance.

Jersey barely manages a word of thanks before the waitress is gone. She grabs her milkshake, hollows her damn cheeks as she sucks on the straw. Her lips detach and she fucking moans.

She points her milkshake in my direction. "Want a sip? It's really good. So. Freaking sweet. Absolutely delish."

I look her straight in the eye. "I'd rather eat your pussy. Pretty sure that's fucking sweet and 'absolutely delish' as well."

She blinks a few times and very slowly retracts the arm holding the milkshake.

Clearing her throat, she says, "I offered you a

taste of my milkshake, not my pussy." The woman surprises me again when the following words tumble from her lips, "Is it really sweet? You know, when you put your mouth between a woman's legs? All those horny guys rattle about eating pussy and I've always wondered if they were bullshitting. Of course, it doesn't help my ex never wanted to give it a try. Funny how I walked in with him shoving his face into a woman's hairy bush, huh? Kinda made me wonder if mine stinks. Oh, great, food. I'm really hungry."

Motherfucking hell. This is what I mean about Jersey being different and rattling–without any shame I might add–about anything that enters her mind.

"Nothing compared to the hunger you flared up inside me," I grumble.

And what the fuck is that shit about her thinking she stinks? Her fucking ex sure did a number on her.

She snorts and gives the waitress a big grin and a thanks while she places our food on the table. I mutter a "Thank you," as well and she leaves with a polite nod.

"Didn't you want any fries?" I question when I glance at the big pile on my plate while Jersey only has a basket with a burger in it with a load of pickles.

Jersey gives a shake of her head. "You've heard about the whole Baton slash Benedict situation, right?"

This woman always keeps me on my toes, switching topics like she just did.

"Yeah. Baton was badly injured, they terminated the trackers, he let himself drop into the sea and Benedict took his place until he bellowed it all out in the parking lot for everyone to hear when that prospect died right in front of him. Traumatizing for the fucker. For everyone I reckon."

Placing the burger back on her plate, she slowly chews and wipes her mouth with a napkin. "Then they took Benedict and Ellory asked me to turn the tracker back on. And that's when I saw something weird about Baton's tracker."

"Is it possible to turn a tracker back on once it's been terminated? It could give false data. I've read somewhere–"

"Stop." She points a slice of pickle in my direction. "For one, you're talking to me and you are able to tell me exactly where you read it, what the page number was, the title of the magazine, if it was a magazine, and recite the statistics. Hell, as a kid every sentence you would start with 'statistics say'. Anyway, my point is…I wondered the same thing but it was worth trying and it worked, okay? No backfire or incorrect data or fail to start back up and function. The only weirdness was the data after it was terminated. And I know for a fact the tracker was terminated completely since the only data retrieved was about a day's worth so it was tampered with and maybe even completely removed and destroyed."

"The twelve-hour data window?" I question, knowing what this must be about since there is some kind of failsafe where the tracker stores data for the next twelve hours in case the tracker is terminated by let's say a kidnapper or something. "And you're sure it added a few extra hours because that sometimes happens due to the wide window of restoring data after the fact so it could merely be an extra few hours added without being tampered with."

"Yep, I know, but it's the coordinates the tracker transmitted during all the data that's interesting," she quips and shoots me a grin and sinks her teeth into her burger.

I take a few bites from mine and wait for her to continue.

"The whole dropping into the sea is consistent with the coordinates. But then it moves and it ends up in a clinic and the last few hours the tracker's signal comes from a hotel."

I shove the rest of my burger into my mouth and wipe my lips with a napkin. If what she discovered is true then there's only one conclusion.

"The fucker might still be alive," I state.

She reaches out and snatches two fries from my plate and right before she shoves them into her mouth she says, "That's what I'm thinking and what we're going to find out."

"The clinic first then the hotel?" I guess, knowing this woman has worked cases for the MC she's a part of; she's by no means a rookie when it comes to investigations.

"Yes, but we have a long road to travel. If we could make an overnight stop, I could see if I can hack into the clinic's system and try to gather information if anyone was treated for anything that day. Unless they work with an old system of manual filing."

"Or if he's managed to keep his visit to the clinic under wraps, then we won't find a trace," I finish for her and polish off my second burger.

She snatches the last of my fries and asks, "Did you pack a bag or do we have to swing by your place to get a few things first?"

"When Archer texted me about a new case he said to meet him here with an overnight bag." I check my watch. "I have to be somewhere in an hour but that won't take more than five or ten minutes, max."

"Do you need me to wait here or come with you?"

"You can come with. I only have to observe something from a distance and then we can hit the road. Archer drop you off or do you have a car here?"

"Dropped me off." She tilts her head. "If you have issues with having me on the back of your bike, I could get my own bike while you handle your thing and be back here within the hour."

The thought of having this woman on the back of my bike spikes some irrational questions, mostly because it causes my dick to harden to the point of pain.

"I've never had a woman on the back of my bike," I answer gruffly. "I don't have an issue with you."

"Sweet. Your bike looks and sounds stunning and I've been wondering how it feels. Now I get to have it between my legs," she blurts and grins but the words she just threw out process in her brain turning her cheeks flaming red as her gaze hits the table.

Fuck, she's cute. My head tips back and laughter rips out. Something hits my face and when I glance at my lap I notice the wrapping paper of a burger she just threw at me.

"Shut it. I'm gonna pay the bill. Archer is footing this one since we're working a case." She doesn't allow me to say anything in return but dashes up and stalks toward the counter.

I stand and grab her backpack to meet her and we walk outside to my bike.

"I took a case yesterday and I need to check out something my client mentioned." I think of a way to tell her this and it makes me pause.

I never take other people's feelings into consideration so why the fuck do I care now? This is business. I have my own company where I take cases from proving infidelity to consulting with the police. My expertise has no limitations and I'm very thorough. It's also why Archer hires me on a regular basis.

It's a little fucked up because I belong to another MC and with Archer hiring me, these days it feels like I have two presidents. It's also why Archer has offered me the Broken Deeds MC patch several times.

I've always turned him down but I know for damn sure he won't be offering it to me again. Mostly because he flat-out told me after the incident in church where Jersey almost hit me.

I should have watched my words back then but I didn't know what she endured with her ex, but I do now. Somehow my brain is telling me Jersey is more than a mere woman walking this earth. It's for this reason I carefully pick my words while I shove her backpack in one of my saddle bags and raise my head to face her.

"I'm working on a missing person case but infidelity is also involved. If the subject is too raw, I could–"

"Don't be silly. Now if we were to witness someone getting hit by a truck I would be objecting. That part is still vivid in my brain. But no worries about exposing me to knacks men have, believe me, I'm well aware."

"Not all men cheat on their women. Statistics say–"

"Whoa there, big boy. Don't throw statistics into this. For one, I really don't need to know for when I actually think about opening myself up for another relationship and secondly, I know for a fact not all men are like the asshole who cheated on me. All the bikers of the first generation have showed me as well as Archer, Vachs, and Benedict. All of them have an old lady who they respect and adore. Maybe I was too trusting because of it, whatever. Life lessons are hard, right? So, missing person, eh? Mind sharing more details? I could help you on this one too since we're already tied up for the next couple of days with Baton's case. You know, give you a woman's perspective on things."

"You're not too trusting, the fucker was an asshole who wasn't worthy of something so perfect," I snarl, hating to hear how she thinks it was her fault for being too damn trusting.

She simply rolls her eyes. "Whatever. Details, Austin, or aren't you going to let me help you?"

I rub a hand over my inked, bald head. "I never work with a woman, and for sure as fuck handle all my company cases myself."

"Fine." The single word comes out without any emotion but I can see the disappointment written clearly on her face.

Releasing a deep sigh, I give in. "The woman who hired me is the mother of the missing person. Her daughter is married to some fancy stock trader. He didn't report her missing and when the mother showed up to ask where her daughter was he told her she wanted to take a short vacation."

"Weird. Do you think he's lying and that he killed her? And what do you need to check first? Anything I can help with?"

Her excitement is making the corner of my mouth twitch.

I straddle my bike and tell her, "The mother said her son-in-law likes to cheat using hookers: even gave me the name of the street he likes to pick them up on like clockwork. It was something her daughter found out right before she went missing."

"Christ, that's twisted," Jersey mutters and slides on behind me.

Her arms go around my waist and her boobs are locked tight against me. I swallow hard at the new feelings flowing through my veins. Hot with a burning need and it feels damn good. It should freak me the fuck out, but it doesn't.

The only issue with this shit is acting on it. And though I know I want nothing more than to have her pussy–like I bluntly told her–I should stay away. I was born into Areion Fury MC and wear my colors with pride, like my father also still does.

Jersey might not be wearing a cut but she's been born into the life. No matter if she took a break and just came back; she dove right into working for the MC again. Needless to say, if we ever cross the line it would make two MCs collide.

It's inevitable. I will fuck up. I'm not able to open up to my damn emotions like others and always look at shit differently. And women? Overload of emotions and their actions are involved with them as well. It's probably why women always walk away from me; I keep stepping on their feelings. And no matter how badly I want Jersey, I don't want to fucking hurt her.

Not her. Never her.

I let the bike roar to life underneath me and allow myself to revel in the feel of her on the back of my bike. The first woman who had the privilege, but there's a timer on it along with restrictions.

Not that any restrictions ever had any effect on me. Nothing did; until her.

CHAPTER THREE

JERSEY

I've been on the back of my father's bike innumerable times. But this right here? This is different. For one my cheek is pressed up against the patch of Areion Fury MC. But most of all it's the excitement running through me because it's laced with a dose of lust and desire.

My fingers brush against his naked abs and I tighten my hold. We've only travelled for a few minutes when he brings the bike to a stop. He doesn't get off but hits the kickstand with his boot and cuts the engine.

The streets aren't crowded. There are four

women across the street, standing on the corner and glancing around while chatting to one another. Cars slowly drive by but no one is stopping. The women's eyes land on us and I can tell they are chatting about us.

Austin curses and pats my leg. "Get off the bike, babe."

I do as he says and hop onto the sidewalk.

Austin takes my hand and pulls me toward him. "Straddle the bike and face me, wrap your legs around me."

"What?" I squeak and gape at the man who must have lost his mind.

"I need to keep my eyes on those women and I can't if they keep staring at us and wondering why we're standing here gawking at them. If you wrap your legs around me, I can bury my face into your neck and watch them while they think I'm sexing you up."

"Well, you would be," I deadpan and swallow hard at the visual this man just planted inside my head.

A sly grin spreads his face. "You offered to help me more than a few times."

I glance at the women across the street and they are now all focused on us. Shit. I let out a frustrated growl and straddle the bike while facing Austin, sliding my legs around his thick, muscled waist.

His hands grip my ass cheeks and I gasp at the way he kneads them and pulls me tighter against him. My arms fly out and I grip his back as his head falls to the crook of my neck. He slowly inhales and tips his head slightly back to let his chin rest on my shoulder.

"Much better," he rumbles. "Great cover."

"Glad to be of assistance," I grumble and try very hard not to move.

The hard part being a major element here because my pussy is plastered to his front and there's something seriously large growing between us.

"Stop grinding your pussy against my cock," Austin whisper growls hot against my ear.

"You're the one holding my ass and keeping me in place. I'm just trying to get comfortable,"

I mutter in return. "And what the hell are you packing? A pair of socks? A roll of peppermints? It's unnatural to have something this big in that place."

Shit. Why do I always ramble out the first thing that comes to mind?

Austin's body shakes with laughter. "Not my fault you're feeling a real man for the first time, babe. But I'm honored."

"Oh, shut it," I huff but deep down I have to admit he's right.

The handful of sexual experiences I had weren't all excitement and pleasurable. My body has never tingled on impact like what happens when Austin touches me, and for sure I've never felt something as big as he is plastered against my pussy.

"Here he comes," Austin mutters and I shift slightly to be able to glance in the direction of the women across the street.

I'm thankful for the change because I feel flustered and my mind is diving off the deep end, wandering what it would be like to be taken by this man. Yes, I said taken because it wouldn't simply be "having sex." Not when his hands are still gripping my ass in a way I can only surrender to his guidance.

One of the four women breaks free from the group and leans in to place her forearm on the car that's stopped along the curb.

"Why do they always go for the redheads?" I wonder out loud.

"Statistics say–"

"You need to shut your piehole with your mathematical analysis. What you should say is that men just have a hard-on for redheads. All while every woman has a pussy and tits, no surprise there, it's–"

"Wet pussy is wet pussy. Whatever rips the cum out. Classy, Jers." Austin chuckles. "Nils wants to get his dick wet with a redhead's pussy."

I take a good look at the woman, noticing a small tattoo on her ankle and wondering how she can balance herself on those high heels. I let my gaze slide up. Breast enlargement for sure, and I'm guessing it isn't the only fake thing about her.

"It's a wig."

"Are you sure?" Austin questions while the woman gets into Nils' car and they drive off.

The car is out of sight and I lock my eyes with Austin, our faces inches apart.

My breath gets caught in my throat and I barely manage to croak, "Yeah."

A grin slides over his face and it's then I realize the man has actually laughed, chuckled, and smiled more today than I've seen him do for as long as I've known him. And that's a long-ass time. His grip on my ass tightens and it ignites a surge of lust to freely flow through my veins.

"Fuck, you feel good." His voice is a raw rumble.

One of his hands leaves my ass but the sudden smack catches me by surprise and makes me squeak.

The asshole laughs and orders, "Come on, babe. Warm my back, not my cock."

I instantly untangle myself and shove his chest while I step off. "Who's the classy one now? And quit calling me babe. I'm not a hang-around or club pussy. Hell, you're not even wearing the right colors for my liking."

He growls low in his throat but I ignore his rude ass and straddle the bike, this time keeping my hands on my thighs. Another growl rumbles from him and he reaches back to snatch my wrists, pulling me tightly against him and making me lace my own fingers against his bare six pack.

"Never risk your own safety, Jers. Even if you're pissed at me." He pats my laced fingers as if to double check they stay locked and fires up the bike.

It's a good thing we can't talk and have a lot of distance to cover. Time passes and it's dark when we finally stop at a hotel to spend the night. I'm the one handling the reservation for the room and am about to suggest we get two rooms but Austin has other ideas.

"One room," he simply grunts to the woman behind the desk and lowers his voice to only tell me, "I won't leave you unprotected."

This part makes me snort. "We're not chasing a serial killer and we're spending the night at a high-class hotel. No protection needed. Two rooms would be–"

A low growl rumbles through his chest and his dark brown eyes swirl with fire. I have to swallow hard and quickly glance away. Crap. Why does he have this effect on me? I'm not scared of him. Sexually intimidated? Maybe. I never used to be, but there's a slight shift in his intentions and my brain jumps to "sexy as hell," and I can't think of him that way.

"One room is fine," I tell the woman and quickly handle all the details.

Once we're in the elevator I whirl around to face him and jab my finger against his chest. "Don't treat me like a helpless chick. I don't need your protection. I can handle myself pretty damn well and we're not handling a hot case where a perpetrator will turn shit around and try to kill us. I might have only worked behind the scenes on cases and have hardly ever been out in the field, but I am your partner. We're investigating a few leads. Treat me like one of the guys, dickwad."

His eyes slide to my finger that's still pressing against his leather cut and slowly slide up to collide with my gaze.

"Fine," he grunts and mutters underneath his breath, "Not sure if you're gonna appreciate it, but you asked for it."

"What the hell does that mean?" I snap.

He simply shrugs and keeps his eyes forward. The doors slide open and we get off the elevator and stroll to our room. Once inside I head for the bed and throw my backpack on it before checking out the bathroom.

It's a very large bathroom and the massive tub in the corner looks amazing. There's also a shower in the other corner and I have to say, I've never stayed in a hotel that has a shower and a separate bathtub. My ass is sore and tired from sitting on the back of a bike for hours and I'm in dire need of a long hot bath. Turning the water on, I smile to myself and stroll back to the bed to get some clothes and personal stuff.

My eyeballs almost hit the floor along with my jaw when I see Austin shove his jeans down. His cock is swinging between his legs and holy shit!

He's pierced. Like quadruple pierced, 'I hijacked the hardware store and explored where they are able to shove needles in that part of a human,' pierced, pierced.

"Like being treated as one of the guys? They sure don't gawk like you're doing. You know, guys mainly mind their own business when we have to share a room."

I'm still trying to tear my gaze away from his sparkling dick but I'm failing miserably. Even if I blink slowly, I still can't wrap my mind about the fact this man has piercings for miles. And he's growing hard, it's like watching a flag slowly rise to let the fabric sway in the wind…or in this case letting the heavy metal rock. Wow.

"How many times did it take for the needle work? You didn't do that all in one go, right? That's…wow. I've never seen one let alone a whole pincushion creation. Does that give you pleasure or is it more for the…no, you won't care about giving…would you?"

"Would I what?" The man shifts, making his dick twitch and swing.

All questions and sanity leave my brain and yet again, I can only stare.

"I need a cold shower," Austin grumbles and stalks into the bathroom.

"But I'm going to take a bath," I squeak and wonder what the hell is going on.

How did we go from apologizing to one another in the diner, straddling him so he can watch a guy pick up a hooker while I'm rubbing against his dick, to him openly swinging it in my face? Well, not in my face but most definitely right in front of me. And now he's taking a freaking shower while I'm supposed to be taking my bath.

Screw it. If he's going all dick-swinging naked, I'm going to set my puppies free too. One of the guys would say "tit-swinging," but seriously just thinking about that hurts my breasts. I strip away all my clothes and mentally curse the bastard who thought he'd treat me as "one of the guys."

I stroll to the tub without taking one glance at the corner where the shower is. I'm happy to see it's filled with water and when I bend over to let my fingers slide into it, I can feel it's the perfect temperature.

Grabbing the cherry bodywash, I squirt in a fair amount and slowly step into the tub to let my body sink into the heavenly hot water. I sigh in contentment and close my eyes to relax into the moment. This is what I need; warmth, relaxation, total serenity without any–

"Are you trying to get me killed?" The rough growl is right beside my ear making me surge up and grasp for my racing heart.

"Motherfucker," I squeak. "Returning the favor without telling me the reason why you think I'm trying to kill you?"

My heart is still beating against my ribs when I whirl my head around to shoot him a glare. He's leaning on the tub with his forearms, his face inches from my naked body. Water drops are sliding down his skin. His eyes, though? Flaming hot. They are a vibrant dark brown but they are somehow darker than normal.

"You're naked. Full tits on display, bending over

the fucking bathtub to give me a glance at your sweet pussy and slide into all this wetness moaning in pleasure. Any sane man would snap. So, yes. You're trying to get me killed because Archer gave me a warning back in church when you almost punched me."

"A warning?" I ask in confusion.

"I might have punched him one in the face when you left, that could be a reason too. But his statement about me not breathing when I leave the clubhouse next time was right before he gave me the warning to stay away from you. The club protects all members, especially members' daughters. So, yeah, Jersey. He might be baiting me by throwing us together and now you're in my face, tits and pussy on show."

Anger started to seep into my veins when he casually said how Archer must be baiting him. Me. A mere pawn. Insensitive asshole. Not to mention how he turns things around and basically states I'm the one running around naked for no good reason while he's the one who started it.

I am so freaking pissed there's a huge lump

in my throat preventing me from talking. And I shouldn't talk because my voice will come out shaky as if I'm about to cry and I hate when that happens because it makes me seem weak. And it's not just the anger overtaking me, I'm also hurt he would think so low of me.

Swallowing back the hurt and anger I close my eyes and lean back while I try to grasp onto the serenity of my warm and welcoming bath. But the relaxation doesn't come. My "Zen moment" has been rudely ripped from me but I'm determined to ignore the asshole and keep my eyes closed until I know he's stepped away.

I don't want to give him the satisfaction of seeing me run away from him. He can go fuck himself. And I do hope Archer kicks his ass the next time he takes a swing at him. And really? Austin clocked a president in his own clubhouse because of his own trait of being rude? That doesn't make sense.

I'm still trying to block everything out–and failing miserably–when I hear a deep sigh. The faint sound of footsteps walking away lets me know

Austin is leaving the bathroom. I mentally count to three hundred before I open my eyes and glance around.

Knowing I'm alone, I pinch my nose and fully lean back into the water, drowning everything out around me. All the bikers of Broken Deeds MC might have a military background, but the fathers made sure their daughters had military training as well.

As a kid growing up, I loved the time and full attention from my father. Knowing how to survive when you have nothing, getting older and sucking up the information how to defend yourself and as a teenager having the skills to kick ass really makes you mentally feel stronger.

I grasp onto that inner feeling and stay under longer. I can easily hold my breath close to two minutes. Well, only if I pinch my nose because I hate the tingles of water when it gets in there. A shadow appears above me and I'm roughly yanked out of the water.

"What the fuck are you doing?" Austin growls.

I shove him away from me and start to slide my hands over my face and hair to get rid of the water sliding down to be able to give the annoying man a glare with a clear vision.

"Taking a fucking bath, what else?"

"You were under for over two fucking minutes," he snaps.

I get up and throw one leg over the tub and grab a towel while I get out of the tub and growl, "I guess I beat my personal record then."

"You're infuriating," the crazy man grumbles underneath his breath.

"And you're an insensitive asshole thinking so low of me. I guess we're on equal footing. Let's agree to shut our mouths unless we have to discuss case related stuff."

I try to dry my body while stalking into the bedroom, wanting to put on clothes and get some work done, all while ignoring this asshole's ass.

I'm successful and am kneading the water out of my hair while walking back toward the bathroom to get rid of the towel when I'm blocked by Austin's massive body. He's only wearing sweatpants and is staring at me with a puzzled look on his face.

Clearly, I'm not able to hang the towel on the hook so instead I ball it up and throw it over his surprised face into the bathroom and spin on my heels to get my brush from my backpack.

I've tamed my hair and am firing up my laptop when I risk a glance at Austin from underneath my lashes. He's still standing in the same spot with his eyes on me as if he's studying a bug.

I grab my notebook and pen and start to dive into finding out details of the clinic where Baton's tracker sent out a signal. The information flows once I've hacked into their system and I'm a bit surprised to find information this freely though it did cost me almost an hour.

There is a record of a man being treated with an arm injury and there is an address left by the patient I'm adding to the list of leads to check out tomorrow. I should have dived into this sooner but ever since Archer took over the gavel from his father there have been a few changes when it comes to working for the government.

For one being the fact that some things need to go by the book. Meaning Archer has to mostly justify actions by filing papers and with things like hacking into a clinic to find personal information. Archer has to send either a text or put in a call that they took on a new case.

It doesn't sound like much but that one call or text grants us any means necessary. Of course, we still have to write a full report once the case is solved so we have everything in writing in case there are any after blows. I've heard many bikers complain about paperwork, but they all do it nonetheless.

Anyway, it's the reason why I didn't dive into gathering information right away. I had to wait till I was sure Archer fired off a text with my name to indicate I'm on a case and am allowed to do anything I need to get things done.

Closing my laptop, I turn the page of my notebook–knowing I'll have to share my findings with Austin tomorrow. But for now, I'm still ignoring his annoying ass. I need a few minutes to clear my brain before I get some sleep and start to sketch an idea of a doll that popped into my head.

It's one of the rare things where I find my peace; designing weird dolls. And with it comes the part where it also earns me a truckload of money so it's a win-win. In this case I'm designing a new doll to keep my sanity intact, knowing I have to work with this asshole I'm sharing a room with for the next couple of days.

But the good thing is, it's also motivation to solve this case as soon as possible. And with the details I just read about the man's injury? Baton is very much alive. Which also proves the fact all men are assholes and only think about themselves.

CHAPTER FOUR

AUSTIN

She's a damn puzzle with missing pieces. And I don't mean it the way it sounds; it's just fucking intriguing to search for the missing pieces or let my mind fill in the blanks. I know she never acts the way I expect her to but she shocked the hell out of me when she walked into the bathroom fully naked a few hours ago.

Naked. Full, delicious looking tits on show, curvy thighs and an ass to dream about; this woman is a dream-worthy treasure for any man. No. Not just any man because the thought of anyone else but my hands roaming her body ignites fury like nothing

I've ever felt swirl inside my chest.

Another thing that doesn't make any sense. She's off-limits and no woman has ever pulled on my thoughts, emotions, whatever. Fuck. Till now I thought I wasn't able to tap into my emotions without fucking everything up, but again–Jersey out of anyone else–she shoves it right into my face.

And I can't complain about it either. Okay, maybe a little bit since I wasn't lying when I told her Archer gave me a clear warning. Though, I told him straight to his face warnings are there for people who heed them. I don't fit any standards nor will I ever. And threatening me to stay away won't work since he keeps hiring me. And what does that fucker do? He damn well hires me to work with her on a fucking case.

She's sleeping on the bed with her clothes on but I know what's hiding underneath. It's branded into my brain thanks to my photographic memory. And now I've been staring at her for hours. First watching her work and then she started to scribble in a notebook. Eventually she moved over to the bed and laid her head on the pillow and fucking fell asleep in the blink of an eye.

I can never get to sleep like that; just lay your head to rest and sleep. How the fuck does she do it? I mean, my mind runs overtime when I close my eyes. So, now I'm a creeper who watches her sleep for hours on end while getting none myself.

I am wondering what she was doing in her note-pad and my eyes slide to it. Checking it out would be a breach of privacy but she's already pissed at me anyway. Decision made, I stroll over to the bed and carefully pick the item up.

Stalking back to the chair, I plunk down and glance up to see she's still sound asleep. It's early morning and I have no clue if she's an early riser. I open the notebook on the page last used and see a sketch of a weird looking doll. The corner of my mouth twitches when I see it has either three legs or she drew him a dick that reaches way past his knees, piercings from tip to root. The thing is inked all over and has buttons instead of eyes.

Normal dolls have arms and a head in the right

proportions but this one has massive biceps and extremely thin forearms. The head? Triple the size and the way it states above the figure "A-hole," I'm fairly sure she was inspired by me while designing this.

The corner of my mouth twitches. I know her mother has her own company in designing and creating stuffed animals. She's so damn good at it she's even hired by the movie industry who request real looking animals to be used on screen for if they need a dog for instance to get hit by a car and such.

The detailed sketch and pattern in her notebook makes me think Jersey creates them in real life. If she doesn't, she absolutely should because something this extraordinary can be exclusive and sell really well. Curious if there's more, I turn the page and stumble onto her notes, the ones she was clearly making when she was doing research on her laptop.

My eyes catch the address she scribbled down and I mentally curse. This shit can't be real. I know for a fact Jersey was checking if she could tap into the clinic's archive to see if there were any details about Baton being treated.

Her notes above the address are about an injury to the arm along with some other facts of his injuries and from what I can tell none of those are life threatening. They are however severe enough to disable him and I'm fairly sure Baton lost the use of his arm.

And the address he gave as a reference for a checkup? It's from one of my president's daughters. Makayla, one of his twin daughters to be specific, who moved out of state to become a fucking doctor. It's a no-brainer for me; we've found Baton.

Well, at least I found someone who knows where the fucker is. It makes perfect sense since Makayla loves the sea and heads out whenever she can with her boat to go diving. She must have seen him drop from the helicopter and fished him out of the water. Fuck. That is one hell of a coincidence.

I close the notebook and put it back exactly the way it was. Fishing my phone out of my pocket, I text my prez for his daughter's number, telling him I need it for a medical question only she would be able to answer and that I'll explain later. My phone instantly shows a reply with the number.

One more glance at Jersey shows me she's still sleeping. I open the sliding door to the balcony and step out for some privacy. It only takes three rings for Makayla to pick up. I know it's early and hearing her sleepy voice gives me the impression I woke her up but I don't fucking care.

"Makayla, Austin here. We need to talk because we have one serious fucking problem. For a chick who moved out of state to leave the MC behind, I'd say you're doing a shitty job by pulling us into another MC's club business, don't you think?" I make sure to keep my voice to a minimum but loud enough for Zack and Blue's daughter to know I'm onto her major fuck-up.

"I don't know what you're talking about. I haven't been to the club in years, Austin. How could I be pulling you guys into another MC's business while I'm living my own damn life?" she hisses in return and I clearly hear a man's voice in the background.

"Put Baton on the fucking phone, Makayla," I snap.

There's a sharp intake of breath before the line is muted by I'm guessing her hand while murmurs flow into my ear.

The line clears and I hear a baritone voice grunt, "Austin, we need to talk."

"Yeah, we do." I glance at my watch and count the hours I need to get shit done. "I'll swing by her place within six hours."

"See you then," Baton replies but I need for him to know.

"You and I Baton, no fucking running or I'll track you down and haul your ass to the clubhouse of Broken Deeds MC myself and not give you the opportunity to explain. Okay? Because I am giving you the choice to talk to me before I make up my mind and report back to Archer who gave me a lead to follow up on, understood?"

"Thanks, man. Appreciate you giving me the choice what you'll be reporting," the fucker says with gratitude in his voice.

I grunt and end the call. Fuck if I let him have a choice in what I'll be reporting back. I always give all the details when I'm hired to do a job and I do my fucking job by giving everything I can to solve it. Including lying to a fucker so he won't run.

Stepping back into the room, I close the balcony door and shove my phone back into my pocket. There's only one more thing left to do and that's crush the woman's feelings before me. I can't take her with me tomorrow since technically one of Areion Fury is now involved in hiding Baton. A clusterfuck, that's what it is.

I take out my phone once more and text Archer to let him know there's a break in the case and that I'm going to wrap it up while Jersey will be returning home in a few hours. My last line in the text is to give credit to Jersey for being the one who put it all together and how I'll explain when I get back.

Shoving my phone into my pocket, I once more grab her notepad and shove it into my backpack along with her laptop. I'll return them to Archer when I get back, but for now, I don't want her to find out who the address belongs to. She clearly hasn't run the address yet, otherwise she would have said something.

Closing my backpack, I let my gaze slide to Jersey again. My heart skips a fucking beat due to a mixture of shock and being caught when I stare into her caramel eyes because she's sitting up and is wide awake.

"What are you doing?" she snaps.

Fuck. Everything is set into motion and I really wanted to take an hour to mentally prepare myself for what I'm about to do. Because I know for a fact she's going to feel bypassed, betrayed, stabbed in the fucking back, and all that shit.

And she's right. I'm an asshole but this is something that has to be done. And strangely enough, it's already killing me because my chest feels as if someone is sliding fingers around my heart and is trying to yank it out through my ribs.

"We need to talk," I grunt and stalk to the bed.

Her eyes go to my backpack before they land on me. "Ya think? But first you need to give me my stuff back."

"I told Archer you cracked the case and that you're going home since I'm handling the wrapping up part."

"The fuck you are," she snarls and gets up, walks right over the mattress to tower over me. "Give. Me. My. Stuff. Back."

The way her eyes are practically spitting fire, hair all over the place, and her face flustered from anger is sexy as fuck and I'm instantly rock hard.

It's for this reason I huskily reply, "Or what, babe?" Knowing it will aggravate her more by adding the babe she mentioned she hates me using on her.

I have one microsecond to think when she launches herself at me. With my hands filled by this stunning goddess, I whirl us around and have her pinned to the bed with my body. Both wrists locked above her head; rendering any of her actions useless.

"Bad move, sweetheart," I whisper in her ear and have to dodge her snapping teeth when she turns her head and growls in frustration.

Shifting my hips, she goes completely still when my cock creates friction against her pussy. Her leggings and my sweatpants are only thin layers between us. I shift both her wrists to be able to keep them pinned with one hand, allowing me to slide the other in between our bodies.

Rubbing her pussy I watch how her face contorts with pleasure. Eyes never leaving mine while lust seeps in. A moan tumbles over her plump lips and her leggings are fucking drenched to my touch. Her arousal is wafting around me and it entices the need to have her.

"Austin," she gasps when I keep circling her clit, building her pleasure.

"What is it, sweetheart? Want me to make you come?"

"Yes," she growls out the word in anger and it makes me click my tongue.

"Now, now, that's no way to treat the man who wants to worship your pussy and give you the pleasure you crave."

"Give it already instead of rambling your mouth," she once again growls out the words.

I push myself upright and leave her body completely. She's staring at me, wide eyed. I want to get inside her so damn bad but I refuse to let her demand shit; I'm in control, always.

Shoving down my sweatpants, I palm my hard cock and give it a tight squeeze, brushing my thumb over the large barbell that's coming out of the slit. With my twisted emotions and feelings, I've added more and more piercings to relish in the way I can tug and spike the balance between pleasure and pain.

"Get naked and on your elbows and knees if you want me, Jersey. And I'm only going to offer you once so no back talk, understood?"

She shoots me a glare but I swear she moves as if her ass is on fire. And I make sure it is once my handprint will decorate her lush curves because she's displayed exactly how I asked with my next breath.

I can't wait to be inside her but first I lean in and grab her ass, pulling those lush cheeks apart to create the room I need to lick her pussy, clit to ass. And she tastes like a damn dream. Sweet with a salty bite and my mouth waters for move.

Teasing her clit with one hand, I spear her pussy with my tongue and balance between licks and sucks until she's pushing back into my face, desperate for release. Moans mixed with my name on a plea fill the air and when I shove one finger deep to rub a spot inside her, she clamps down on me in rapid waves.

The sounds flowing through the air make my balls tingle with the craving to ride the same bliss and it's the reason I tear my mouth from her and instantly replace it with my cock. I grip her hips and thrust forward, hard enough to knock her off her elbows and make her faceplant into the mattress.

She scrambles up when I pull out and when I throw my hips forward again she's expecting my hard assault on her pussy and pushes right back with the same force. Fucking hell it's as if she's made for me.

Tight. Wet. Taking all of my cock without one complaint and I'm telling you, that's never happened. Women might want a large cock but in reality, it's hard to take unless there's enough preparation.

But not with this woman. She's so damn primed it's a match in every way because she can't get enough and I damn well know it's due to the fact she's pushing back on my cock. She's feeding me her pussy as if it's starving for more. The moans of pleasure also give it away but mostly? It's her begging for more.

Maybe not begging, more like demanding when she growls, "Rotate. Surge. Fuck, Austin, give me more. Harder. You feel so good. Fuck. Yes. There. Again. Yessss….I'm gonna…I need…yes." The rest of her words are incoherent when she falls into bliss.

I'm about to follow her and it's then I realize I didn't wrap up. I've never fucked anyone bare and I know I should pull out because I don't know if she's on the pill or not but the choice is taken from me when her pussy spasms some more, ripping the cum right from my body.

White hot bliss surges through my veins and I actually see stars so damn bright it makes my brain short circuit. I'm not able to hold my own weight and let myself collapse on top of her. Jersey grunts and I turn slightly but keep a hand on her hip to keep her pussy wrapped around my cock.

Fuck. That was amazing. Best pussy I've ever had for sure. And I'm not saying it because it's been a long damn time since I got my dick wet; I know for certain it's Jersey and the effect she has on me. Our breaths come out choppy and I can feel her racing heart.

"I need another hour of sleep before I have the strength to argue with you," Jersey mumbles.

"Woman," I growl. "If this is your version of arguing, I'm available for arguing every damn minute of the day."

"Yeah, yeah," she mutters sleepily. "Like I said, in another hour...then we'll–" Her words are cut off by mumbling until a soft snore fills the air.

I can't help but chuckle and it makes me slip out from her pussy. Regretfully, I shift off the bed and glance back to see Jersey is still sound asleep. Either I fucked all the energy right out of her or she's still tired since it's quite early in the morning.

Stalking into the bathroom, I quickly handle my business and very quietly get dressed. Once I'm ready I take one last look at the woman I now know holds my heart but won't ever be mine. I slide out of the room and gently close the door of not only the room, but also any chance at a relationship with the woman who will forever fill my dreams.

Once I'm on my bike and have hit the road for a few hours, I make a stop by the side of the road and shoot a text to Jersey, letting her know I'll give her laptop and notebook to Archer once I'm back. I deliberately turn my phone off and continue my way to meet up with Baton and Makayla.

The sun is shining bright when I finally park my bike in front of Makayla's house. I notice the curtains move and when I'm almost at the door, it swings open. It's fucked-up to see a man standing there who looks exactly like Benedict but is in fact his twin, Baton.

A fucker who asked his twin to take his name and make it seem he lives forever, as if that's even remotely possible. Not to mention, making Benedict think Baton jumped into the sea to fucking die. I have no respect for this man and it's for this reason I knock my shoulder into his and enter the house of my president's daughter without so much as a hello.

Makayla's eyes are on the floor when she says, "Hey, Austin."

"Don't fucking hey me if you're hiding a biker from another fucking MC. One who gave his twin the fucking burden of his death while kissing his own life and name goodbye to live the life of his brother. Sentencing Benedict's own identity to die along with it. I have no good word or thought for you." I whirl around and face Baton. "For the both of you for that matter."

"He did what?" Baton grunts.

I glance at Baton and take in his stunned expression.

It makes me snort. "What do you think it took, asshole? You asking him to turn off the tracker, make you live forever, that it wouldn't affect his life? That he would just cut you out of everyone's lives without an explanation? He took your fucking burden and carried it solely on his shoulders until it almost drove him to his own death. And it took a man, a prospect of Broken Deeds, to die right in front of him to snap and spill your fucked-up secret. I don't get it, man. And I couldn't care shit about other people's feelings. But you? You're an insensitive motherfucker who should blackout your ink because you don't deserve to carry that patch. And don't fucking blame shit on your limp arm either."

Baton's face turns to ash.

Good. Let that shit I just spilled kick in.

And to add some more I tell him, "I don't care if you two leave, die, or live here happily ever after. But know I'm leaving here to expose the shit you two have been hiding from both MCs."

I knock once more against Baton's shoulder and walk right out of their house. I should have asked for his reasons, I should have dragged the both of them with me. I should have done loads of things but I'm pissed. And it's not solely about them, the shit they did, or the fact Baton is alive.

It's because my heart feels heavy for what I did to Jersey this morning. And that's on them too, but it's mostly on me. Except, there's nothing I can do to change what I did or the blowback that's hitting me harder than ever.

I straddle my bike and fire it up. The hours on the road I have ahead of me probably won't clear my head the way I normally enjoy to tear up the road and the relaxing freedom it gives me. It feels more like tearing up my heart with every mile that passes.

CHAPTER FIVE

A few weeks later

JERSEY

"Hey, you. Welcome back." Beatrice gives me a warm smile and points at a chair.

I place my bag on the floor next to it and plant my ass on the seat.

With a deep sigh I give her the words, "Thanks. I'm beat after driving for over five hours. Everything is still in my truck and I am happy I could bring all my belongings back in one go."

"I'm glad you managed to sell your condo and close that particular chapter of your life. Time to start over, right here with us where you belong." She holds up her mug. "Coffee? I just made some."

I grimace and shake my head. "No, thanks. I've been feeling woozy all day."

"Have you eaten yet? The long drive and packing your stuff and moving, hell, everything you've been doing the last few weeks has been draining. You need to take better care of yourself. Shall I get you some orange juice?"

A chuckle slips over my lips. "Thanks, mom," I mock. "But no, I'll grab something to eat and drink later. I want to talk to Archer first."

She sits across from me and places her mug on the table in front of her. "He's in his office. I gather you want to ask him for a case to put your teeth in? Are you still angry for what happened with–"

"Don't mention that asshole's name," I growl.

Beatrice grimaces. "Sorry. He can be a real ass but you also have to give it to the man, it was a delicate situation and he made sure to let my old man know you were the one who solved and closed the case. He went out of his way to–"

"To shove me in a corner and leave me there without looking back?" I snap, barely keeping the words "after he fucked me," inside my head.

I'm such a freaking idiot. A bigger one for only realizing afterward we didn't use a condom. I used to take the pill without missing one, but with the abrupt move here with what happened with my ex, I forgot to take most of my personal belongings and I stopped taking it. It's not like I was going to have sex any time soon anyway. And to top it off, Austin is a single biker who clearly likes sex with all those piercings decorating his dick.

I make a mental note to get tested because with the shit I've had to deal with these past few weeks it slipped my thoughts. I selfishly replaced everything with anger while I should have been thinking about my health. I just had my period before we had sex. Maybe pregnancy is a slight chance, STD, though? Yeah…I need to get myself tested as soon as possible.

"No. You're making this too personal, Jersey. He's Areion Fury and recognized the address of one of the daughters of his president. He called her and confirmed Baton was indeed alive and had been living with one of his MC all this time. It's MC to MC, Austin being in the middle, he took it upon himself to make sure everything went smoothly."

I surge up and embrace the anger filling my body. "You're on his side because you're Areion Fury MC and Broken Deeds MC too. Right in the middle like he is."

Beatrice's eyes widen before they narrow. Guilt instantly hits me and I know I'm taking my anger out on her.

"Sorry," I mutter and sink down onto the chair, placing my head in my hands while I balance my elbows on the table.

"You're right, I'm the daughter of Areion Fury's VP, nothing can change that fact. But first and foremost, I'm also the old lady of the president of Broken Deeds MC. This is where my loyalty lies, but this also means I understand Austin's actions better than anyone else. Though, I also know Austin and the kind of man he is. He wouldn't have made an effort to plead a case for someone else before doing his job. He's a practical man who thrives on schedules, statistics, technicalities, clean and basic shit. He's not a man who demands my old man credit another person for their actions as well. Not to mention texting me daily for updates about you. It's annoying to say the least and very unlike him."

"What the hell?" I squeak. "I hope you haven't told him shit."

"Language, Jersey. I might not have my kids near me but I'd appreciate keeping the words shit and fuck to a minimum. It's hard enough with Archer running his mouth along with everyone else. And no, I didn't tell him anything other than the fact you're a strong woman who can take care of herself without him checking up on you. But that doesn't stop him from trying. I don't know why either because he's never been like this. Heck, I can honestly say I've never texted with him nor did I have the need. He's a friend because we grew up together in the same MC but he's always been a loner. Any reason why he's being obsessive about needing to know if you're okay?"

I rub my eyes and release another sigh. I'm

absolutely fried from driving half the day. Hell, I'm fried from working my ass off for the last few weeks to handle my past and make the move here indefinitely. It's been a good way to keep my mind busy and ignore the whole Austin situation.

A lie. Ignoring the Austin situation has been futile.

"We had sex. I woke up to an empty hotel room, phone ringing and Archer telling me to come home and thanks for cracking the case and solving it. And how Austin was going to wrap up the loose ends."

"What the fuck?" Beatrice growls and it actually puts a smile on my face.

"Language, Bee," I fake scold and bark out a laugh but it quickly turns into a sob and I swallow hard to push down all my emotions. "It was more than taking the case from me to wrap it up himself. I feel betrayed. Left. Disposed. I don't know…used? Not enough for sure."

I stare at Beatrice and there's pity written all over her face and I hate it. If these few weeks of clearing out the old and putting the past behind me has taught me anything, it's the fact that I have to stop caring about everything else and focus on myself.

Plastering a smile on my face I tell her, "It's why I want to ask Archer for a case. I want to work but mainly I want to solve it by myself."

Beatrice nods. "You were cheated out of that one."

I'm glad she gets it. "Yes, I was."

She grabs her phone and lets her fingers slide over the screen. "Archer asked if you can meet him in his office. And this is by no means me interfering or the president doing a favor for his old lady… it's–"

I don't care what it is because I'm thankful to have her understanding and it's for this reason I cut her off by rushing toward her and giving her a hug.

"Thank you."

"Yeah, yeah…go, he's waiting." She squeezes me one more time and pushes me away. "Thanks for trusting me, Jersey. And I wish I'd known what he did. But I'm also happy I only told him you were busy with moving and packing and stuff. It basically means you were moving on without a hitch."

I nod and smile once more. I snatch my backpack from the floor and head for Archer's office. Rasping my knuckles on the door, he barks out his words for me to enter.

Pointing at the chair he lifts his chin and says without looking at me, "Sit. I'm in the middle of something but I hear you want to work on a case, right? Good, I have some new ones added to the pile and I could use a skilled pair of hands."

His laptop is open, he's holding his phone in one hand while he glances through a file with the other and a large stack of files is on the corner of his desk. I'm about to say something but a photograph catches my attention and I lean forward to take it from his hand.

"Is this a new case?"

I take in the woman, bound by hands and feet, throat sliced and it seems like someone cut out her tongue and poked her eyes out.

"Yeah, just landed on my lap. Three dead women so far, all the same M.O."

"I want this one," I instantly state and hand him the photograph back.

Archer places his phone back on his desk and folds his arms in front of his chest. I just know he's going to turn me down and give me some low-profile case instead.

"You owe me," I snap. "I can handle this one like anyone else here and you know it."

He actually winces and his eyes slide to his phone. Maybe he's thinking about the text Beatrice sent him, even if I have no clue what she said. He releases a deep breath.

"Fine. But murder cases are always handled in pairs and you know it. I'll give you lead on this but Wyatt is your partner. You keep him in the loop and when you need backup you make him go with you."

I can feel a huge smile spreading my face. "Thank you, I won't let you down. And just to be sure, I have your word no one is going to take this case away from me, right? It's mine."

"Jersey." Archer gives me a sympathetic look. "What happened had nothing to do with you. Austin handled it correctly. In fact, he didn't have a choice and did what any brother would have done. Hell, the guy earned a marker from me by doing so and I don't hand them out lightly. Even if I hired him to do the damn job."

Yada, yada, yada. My brain mutes out the "Austin is awesome," speech and I tune back in when he starts to mention Baton.

"We never would have known he might be alive if it wasn't for you. You came to me, you're the one who found the leads and solved it by getting the address. It doesn't matter Austin wrapped it up so you could return home. And to be honest? If I were there, I would have done the same thing. Except I wouldn't have put Baton in his place by merely using words, I would have punched the fucker in the face for what he did. I still can't believe he turned his back on us because he lost the use of his arm and can't ride a bike. What? All life is lost because you can't ride? And then throw your life away, put a heavy weight on your twin only so you can start a whole new life with the help of a newfound friend who happens to be the daughter of another fucking MC president? He's a fucking selfish bastard, that's what he is."

Yikes. I can hear weeks of talking and time hasn't lessened the anger everyone is holding toward Baton. Two days after I got back from waking up alone in that hotel room, Baton came to the clubhouse and went into church. They were tied up in there for a whole day and while the old ladies and I were in the main room, we were able to follow some of the discussion due to the loud bellowing.

Archer growls some muted curses and closes the file in front of me, holding it out for me to take. "But none of it is your concern because you did good. And I know you can handle this case. No worries, Jersey, you have my word. No one will take this case from you: it's yours."

I glance through the file and my eyes fall on what I was looking for, a date. It adds up to the suspicions I had when I saw the photograph of the dead woman.

"Good." A sly grin slides on my face. "I do need one favor but I can also ask Wyatt to do it for me."

"Do what?" His attention is already on both his phone and his laptop.

Though his gaze instantly collides with mine when I tell him, "Call Austin because the woman in the photograph is connected to a missing persons case I know he's been working on. Seeing as it's connected, I would like for him to hand everything over."

"Motherfucker," Archer growls and rubs a hand over his face before he glares at me. "This is about getting back at him, isn't it?"

Hell, yes, it feels good to take a case from Austin, but that's not what this is about.

"Thanks for thinking so little of me, Prez," I snap. "But no, I want to solve this case. I might have recognized the woman in the photograph from when I saw her when Austin and I were checking a lead on his case, but I'm not as petty as you might think. You know damn well everything is about information and leads. And when your mind is triggered you dive in because you're two steps ahead when that happens."

He nods in understanding and points a finger in my direction. "Fucking coincidence or not, it's screwed up. But I also know it puts you at an advantage because there are no leads in this case. Go on, get out of here and find Wyatt. You're taking him with you when you're swinging by Austin's office. I don't want you alone with him."

I'm about to tell him off how I can handle myself but he's showing me the palm of his hand, cutting me off.

"It's for his protection, not yours. You two go head-to-head at every turn. I'm your employer, you work for me and I'm ordering you to take your partner with you, okay? Besides, you're Broken Deeds and heading into Areion Fury territory."

"Fine," I grumble and throw my backpack over my shoulder. Holding up the file I tell him, "Thanks for the case and the trust."

He lifts his chin and places his phone to his ear. A smile spreads my face when I hear Archer snap, "Austin, it's Archer. I'm afraid I have to order you to hand over your notes and information about a case I know you've been working on. I'll send someone by to pick it up."

My cheeks hurt from grinning and I feel so much better already. Well, mentally only. My body feels as if it's running on empty and I really should have eaten some. I find Wyatt in the main room of the clubhouse with a book in his hand. I drop down next to him and the man doesn't even look up from the thriller he's reading.

"You and me, partner," I state. "Archer gave me a case and appointed you as my partner. I will be taking point but I have to swing by Austin's place to pick up information he has and Prez wants you to tag along."

Wyatt closes the book and places it on the table in front of me, turning to fully face me with a shit-eating grin on his face.

"Karma at its best, huh? How the fuck did you manage to land a case in your lap that allows you to steal a case from his hands?"

I hand him the file and he flips it open. He's skimming through the photographs and papers while I tell him what I know.

"When Austin and I had to work together on the Baton case, he was working on a missing persons case of his own. Austin had to check out if the client's suspicions were right, how the husband of the missing woman was cheating on her daughter. We saw how the husband picked up a hooker." I grab one of the photographs from his hands and hold it up. "This was the woman I saw getting into his car. And I checked the date when she went missing, it's the same day."

"Holy fuck. That's one hell of a lead you have there."

I nod at his words. "Let's see if it's a lead that exposes the killer. We also need to see if he's linked to all the other dead bodies."

Wyatt gets to his feet. "Who knows, maybe the man also killed his wife. Quite the coincidence if the fucker is linked with a hooker turning up dead and his wife gone missing, don't you think?"

"Right. But he might as well have picked up the woman, gotten his fill and each of them went their merry way. The missing woman could have re-surfaced or simply left to make a life somewhere else to get rid of her husband. That's for us to find out." I hold up my backpack. "Let me drop this in my room and I'll be ready in a bit. I have to grab an energy bar or something quick to eat, I haven't had much all day."

"You do that and I'll grab the keys of one of the SUVs and wait out front, okay?"

I lift my chin and head for my room. Last week Archer offered me one of the spare rooms in the back. These rooms are used by members of the MC and I could have stayed with my parents in my old room but it makes me feel like a kid who can't han-dle my own life. And with everything that happened I needed my own space.

I told my parents I was going to look for my own space and an hour later Archer was on their doorstep telling me there was a room at the clubhouse for me. I know I have my father to thank for this room and I know they want to keep me here instead of moving out of state again.

Truth is, I'm done with everything that happened in the past. And I might hate working with computers but it's also something I'm really good at. Solving cases is what I've known while growing up along with my mother's passion to create things.

I'm thankful to be able to combine these two things. And I might be staying at the clubhouse for now, but later tonight I'm going to search for a new place near the clubhouse. I just really want my own space. It's not because I'm ungrateful but it's more about getting on my own feet.

This case is one step forward and also a sign toward myself to know I've also left Austin behind me completely. I'm done with all the negativity and feelings; it's time to think about myself for a change.

That reminds me. I grab my phone and contact the clinic to schedule an STD test. Thinking about myself comes with watching my health. Making sure I'm clean and most of all, filled with energy and it's not something I'm feeling right now.

Peering into the refrigerator, I grab a bottle of orange juice and with the first two sips I have to place a hand over my stomach. Shit. Maybe orange juice isn't a good choice to drink on an empty stomach. Grabbing a few crackers, I nibble on those before I head out to face the one person I'm not looking forward to seeing again.

CHAPTER SIX

AUSTIN

My eyes are glued to my phone. I shouldn't torture myself but I can't fucking help it. The picture I took of her gorgeous face, hair spread like a halo to give expression to her stunning beauty is the only thing I have to remember her by.

I don't have to glance at her picture, every single thing about this woman is branded into my brain. Every detail, every inch of her skin, and the taste of her on my tongue. Utter torture. A deep sigh rips from my chest. My mood has been sour from the moment I left her on that bed in an empty hotel room.

I knew I could have handled it differently but

to be honest? What other choice did I have? I needed to make sure the alliance between the two MCs was safe and I had to do it alone. I couldn't risk bringing a Broken Deeds MC to the doorstep of the daughter of a president because I knew how it looked. Hell, I flipped when I realized what those two did.

It's all cleared and handled now, but still…it bugs the shit out of me the way things were left between me and Jersey. I've reached out to Archer, wanting to talk to Jersey but he told me to leave her alone.

I've been asking his wife how she was doing, wanting to soothe my concerns and guilt, but the only thing I found out was the fact Jersey left town to handle her old life and that she would be back later this week.

I should ignore everyone and show up on her doorstep but there's another dilemma about her not having a place of her own. She hasn't been answering my calls or texts, that alone should make me aware she doesn't want to talk to me. But I've never felt this shitty and it's killing me. I don't know what the fuck I should do.

"Stop staring at her picture," I grumble to myself. "That might help."

My eyes slide to the empty dog bed in the corner. I have the same one next to my bed and haven't removed either one. The loss of my dog is another crushing part of my life and it adds to the loneliness that's intensified over the past few weeks.

I shove my phone into my pocket and glance at the clock. I've closed three cases over the past few weeks. I've been working my ass off to keep my brain occupied and other than getting my work done it hasn't done anything to soothe my state of mind.

The only case I have open at this moment is the missing woman. I haven't made a lot of headway with that case other than the knowledge the hubby had been fucking his way through their marriage. The woman could have left town and I wouldn't blame her. The asshole husband deserves to be left in the dirt.

But if she did leave town, she would have left a trail, or at least told her mother and she hasn't yet.

I open the drawer of my desk and grab the file. Going over all the data I gathered can sometimes lead to new leads.

Most of my notes aren't written down and are inside my head. I've gone over everything time and time again and I'm stuck. It bothers the shit out of me because that almost never happens. This can only mean one thing; the woman is dead. First suspect would be the husband. Maybe I need to start treating it like a murder case instead of a missing persons case.

Things would be easier if I was able to work like Broken Deeds MC; use any means necessary. But I can't because I have my own company and am bound by laws I have to stick to. The thought enters my brain to contact Archer but it's then I realize the fucker just called, telling me I need to hand over information about one of my cases and that he'll have someone swing by to collect the files.

My eyes go to the file in front of me. Motherfucker. Why do I only now realize this might be the case he wants to take off my hands? *Because all you think about is Jersey*, my mind easily supplies.

I'm about to call Archer when my doorbell rings. I glance at the monitor to see who is standing on my porch and my heart fucking lurches. Jersey. The woman occupying my brain, the one who ignores all my messages and texts is standing on my porch along with Wyatt, vice president of Broken Deeds MC. *What the hell is going on?*

I hit the button to unlock my front door and see Wyatt push it open. He's been to my house many times over the last few years. We might be from different MCs but with me working with them regularly it's only natural for them to come over to my place when we need a space to work.

I've owned this place for about five years now and I had it built after my own demands. It's located closer to the Broken Deeds compound but that's only because this was the perfect space for what I had in mind.

I like serenity and wide-open space and this piece of land allowed me to build a two-story modern house with wide open spaces. It's also the reason why I have very little to no furniture; only the necessities.

Strolling into the lobby, I meet both Jersey and Wyatt. The fucker has a massive grin on his face while Jersey's face is void of all emotion. I'm not liking the black circles underneath her eyes. It's probably due to working hard and getting everything handled with moving back here.

"You look like shit." The words are out of my mouth before I can swallow them back. "I mean, you look like you could use some sleep."

Her eyes narrow. "What I could use is everything you have about the missing woman case."

My gaze shifts to Wyatt.

The fucker is still wearing a shit-eating grin when he simply says, "You heard the lady. I'm pretty sure Prez called and told you to hand it over."

"He mentioned something about needing information about a case, not about this one specifically," I snap, not liking where this is going. I shift my attention back at Jersey. "You're enjoying this, aren't you? Did you put them up to this? Get back at me because you feel like I stole your case? Which I fucking didn't because I made sure you were given the credit."

"How fucking big of you," she growls in a deadly tone.

"This is not getting us anywhere." Wyatt sighs and places a hand on Jersey's shoulder to pull her behind him and that's when I see red.

"Get your fucking hands off her," I growl.

My hands are curling into fists and I'm a breath away from punching this fuck's face. Wyatt isn't an idiot and removes his hand.

"Jers, wait in the car," Wyatt orders.

"Wait in the…what am I, five? I'm not waiting in the car. Just give us the damn file, Austin. This has nothing to do with you or me: this is about a new case that landed in my lap." Her voice sounds strained and I tear my gaze away from my eyeballing moment with Wyatt.

And it's just in time too because I can barely manage to step forward to catch her. Swooping her into my arms I head for the living room.

"She looks like shit, what the hell is wrong with her?" I bark at Wyatt.

"Hell if I know. Before we left she said something about not eating and headed for her room to grab something."

"Get some juice or a soda from the fridge, anything with sugar is fine," I order and Wyatt heads toward the kitchen.

I have her draped over my lap and gently brush my fingers over the side of her face. Up close I can clearly see she's drained herself. Fucking hell, isn't anyone paying attention around her? Her eyes flutter and when she realizes she's on my lap she starts to squirm and push at my chest.

"Stop struggling," I snap. "You're drained and Wyatt is going to bring you some juice. You're going to drink something and let it settle."

"Let. Me. Go," she hisses.

I clench my teeth and try to offer her another option. "I'm going to put you on the couch but you're going to sit there until I say it's okay to get up." She's about to hiss out some more words but I slowly shake my head. "I won't have you taking another nose-dive again."

She doesn't say anything in reply and I take it as a win. Shifting her off my lap, I place her on the couch and she instantly scoots away but the sudden movement makes her reach for her head again.

"Fucking hell, what did I–"

"What did you do? I don't know, gave me an STD, maybe? I feel like shit so it's possible right? Because you didn't use a fucking condom, asshole," she growls so damn loud her voice bounces off the walls.

"Wow, didn't see that one coming," Wyatt says and releases an awkward chuckle. "Here's your juice, Jers, though I doubt it'll help. Maybe you're pregnant, it would explain your symptoms more than having an itch due to an STD."

"I'm not pregnant," Jersey growls and roughly takes the juice from Wyatt, causing it to slosh over the rim.

I watch in horror when it lands on the floor.

"Oh, fuck," Wyatt mutters underneath his breath.

"I'll get some napkins or something."

"Leave it," I snap and grind my teeth.

"Are you sure? I mean, it turns sticky and–" Wyatt has enough brain cells to cut off his own sentence.

My blood boils and I have to actually close my eyes to take a calming breath. I hate litter, I hate sticky, dirty shit, and I hate people spilling stuff. Everything needs to be clean.

I get to my feet and head into the kitchen. Taking two cloths–one wet and one dry–I head back and start to clean the spot on the floor. I risk a glance at Jersey but she's just watching me with troubled eyes.

When I'm done, I head for the kitchen and hear Jersey whisper to Wyatt to get an explanation. The fucker easily supplies the answer how I'm a bit of a neat freak. Asshole. He should mind his own business.

I walk back into the room and I half expect her to throw the glass and contents to the floor to piss me off, but instead she's holding her hand underneath the glass. I grab a few tissues from the box on the table and hand them to her.

I direct my attention to Wyatt. "Can you leave us? I want to talk to her in private to clear up a few things."

His eyes slide to Jersey. "I don't know if that's such a great idea."

"I don't fucking care what you think," I snap, making the fucker glare at me, but the both of them need to realize one thing. "You want all the info I have on the case, right? Well, it's all in my head because I never write full reports when I'm working on an active case. I may have scattered notes that make no sense to anyone so it's better if I update Jersey by talking her through everything I found."

"You can do that with me right here," Wyatt snaps.

"Or I can refuse," I snap back.

"Or the both of you can shut up and hand me some aspirin because I'm really starting to get a fucking headache with all that growling back and forth."

Wyatt's face washes with sympathy and he squats down. "What do you want, Jers? Maybe he can write everything down and we can swing by tomorrow or–"

"It's fine. I'll listen to what he found out and he'll bring me back to the clubhouse when we're done."

Not that I was going to do what Wyatt offers but it's good to hear Jersey is going to stay with me and relies on me to take her home.

"Okay." His eyes land on me. "You watch yourself, understood?"

"You think it's wise to threaten a brother from another MC?" I snap.

"I don't fucking care who you are or what patch is on your cut. I will always take care of what's–"

What the fuck is he going to say? What's his? Fat fucking chance.

I cut him off by stating, "She's not yours."

"She's Broken Deeds MC," Wyatt snaps.

The corner of my mouth twitches. "Unless she's pregnant, then she'll become my old lady. Areion Fury property."

Wyatt growls but it's cut off by Jersey's bellow, "I. Am. Not. Pregnant!"

"Okay, you know what? I don't do drama and you two are clearly grown up enough to fuck and fix your own damn problems. Jersey, call if you need me to come pick you up. You, keep your hands off her. And Jersey? You better be home in a few hours."

"You're not my father," Jersey grumbles.

Wyatt raises his eyebrow. "Want me to tell my brother what I just heard you guys mention? Because for sure as fuck everyone would flip if they knew this asshole shoved his dick where it didn't belong."

"Out," I growl and get to my feet to kick the fucker out of my damn house.

He holds up his hands. "I'm going. As long as we have an understanding."

I don't say one damn word in reply but keep my eyes pinned on the fucker until the door closes behind him.

I think of how to start but Jersey starts to ramble, "Look, I'm sorry for crashing but I'm fine. I drove for five hours nonstop, have been packing stuff for days, and just sold my condo and moved back. It's a lot to deal with and I might have forgotten to get enough fluids and food in me. I just need some food and a good night of sleep and I also don't care in what order."

Taking the glass from her hand, I reach for the remote and hand it to her. "Go watch some TV, I'll make you a sandwich and then we'll talk."

"You don't need to do that," she starts to object.

"Humor me. Besides, it's the least I can do after leaving the way I did. And just so you know? I fucking hated it and have hated myself every single minute of the day since."

She falls back onto the couch and leans her head into the soft cushions.

"Fine," is all she murmurs and I head for the kitchen.

I take my time to make a sandwich, hoping it's long enough for her to fall asleep. When I stalk back into the living room, I find her curled up with her eyes closed. Placing the sandwich down, I head for the bedroom and grab one of the fluffy blankets my mother bought me. I've never used them but they are coming in handy now.

I cover her up and when I'm sure she's in a deep sleep, I head out and take my bike to make a quick run to the mall. Twenty minutes later I'm walking back into my house and find her still sleeping on my couch.

Taking a picture, I text it to Wyatt with the words, "Haven't had the chance to talk yet. I'm going to let her crash here. I'll bring her back to the clubhouse early tomorrow morning."

All I get back is one single word: fine.

Weeks where my whole body felt tight and my mood was shit and now it's all shifted. I'm not liking the way she has those black circles underneath her eyes but I'm fucking thrilled she's sleeping on my couch.

One thing hitting me today is the fact I want this woman in my life. I should care about the risks but then again, Archer himself married my VP's daughter. Hell, we found Baton shacking up with my Prez's daughter and all they've rambled about was what Baton did by declaring himself dead. Though

Baton and Makayla both state they're just friends and don't have a relationship.

No matter what Jersey and I have to face, I'm sure in the long run shit will settle. First, we need to overcome our differences. Meaning my woman is pissed at me the way I left her in that hotel room all by herself. But I'm sure she can't deny our attraction. We burned the damn sheets.

And yet here I find myself once more, sitting in a chair across from her while watching her sleep. Except this time I'm not thinking about ways to handle a case and handling her. Fuck, no.

This time I'm thinking of ways to get her to stay. Plotting a future. Because one thing is for sure; this captivating, intriguing, and the most stunning woman currently sleeping on my couch is mine. My old lady.

And as soon as I give her those words, I will officially claim her. She might refuse the first time, but I'm a persistent man. Planning the future means long term, and we have all the time in the world.

CHAPTER SEVEN

JERSEY

I slowly awake and yawn while rubbing my eyes. I must have slept for hours because I actually feel a hell of a lot better than…shit. Where am I? Blinking fast I take in my surroundings and notice Austin sitting in a chair across from me.

There's a plate with an untouched sandwich on the table and the turn of events come rushing back to me. Wyatt and I were supposed to get the information about a case. *My case.* I fainted. Ugh. How humiliating.

"Feel better?" Austin questions while he leans forward and places his forearms on his knees.

I stretch my arms above my head and shamelessly groan. I already made a fool out of myself so I might as well enjoy a good stretch after crashing on his couch.

"Actually, I do," I find myself saying.

"I'll make you another sandwich, this one is hours old. Want some coffee?"

"What time is it?" I yawn once more and grab my phone to answer my own question. "Six in the morning?" I gasp. "I slept through the whole afternoon, evening, and night?"

"You did. I guess your body needed it or you allowed yourself to fully relax once you were back with me." The arrogant man shoots me a wink and walks out of the room.

I get to my feet and slowly follow him while I take in my surroundings. Practical, clinical, and clean are the first three words popping into my head to describe this place. The only things in the living room were the couch, two chairs, a table, and a TV.

Remembering the juice incident where Austin cleaned the floor with not one but two cloths is also something I remember all too vividly. I should have known someone with a photographic memory would like to have a clean surrounding. But somehow, I also couldn't picture it with the burly man having a rough beard and not wearing a shirt–just his cut–half the time.

The scent of coffee makes me nauseous. I have to hold my hand on top of my stomach and stop walking.

"Are you okay?" Worry is edged on his face.

"Just a little woozy. Too much sleep and no food, I'm sure."

He grabs a brown paper bag from the counter and holds it out for me to take.

"I bought you something. Least I could do since I should have been the one who brought the condoms. And use them, don't forget that part. But I have to say…you blew my mind and all I could think was burying myself deep. I still do. I'm clean so you don't have to worry about that part. Unless you're not."

"I am. I got tested the same day that asshole

died," I mutter and open the bag to glance inside. "You bought me a pregnancy test?"

"I'm not liking the dark circles underneath your eyes. Pregnancy would make sense with the fatigue and wooziness. If we rule it out you might want to swing by a doctor to make sure you don't have a bug. Some rest would also be–"

"Okay, buddy. Feel free to shut up any time," I grumble and instantly regret my grouchy tone of voice. "Sorry. I'll pee on the damn stick and show you I'm not pregnant. It's just these past few weeks that have been kicking my ass."

I spin on my heel to head for the toilet but freeze because I have no clue where the freaking toilet is.

"Down the hall to your right is a bathroom," Austin informs me and I head this way with the paper bag in hand.

Once inside, I lock the door and take one of the tests out of the bag. Clearly, I've never done this before but the whole "Pee on a stick," doesn't sound hard. I glance over the images showing how it works and quickly handle everything.

And now we wait.

I grab my phone and decide if I should stay here or get a sandwich. My stomach takes this moment to rumble and I guess some food does sound perfect. Leaving everything next to the sink, I head back into the kitchen and find Austin cutting pickles.

Without thinking I stick my fingers into the jar and snatch one of the pickles. I absolutely love them. Any time of day really. Austin must have known because I ordered double pickles when we grabbed some food at the diner.

"Not pregnant, eh?" Austin chuckles and lifts his chin at my empty hand.

I roll my eyes. "You sound a little too eager for my liking. But no, I always had a craving for pickles."

"I am eager. You're my old lady so pregnant now or any time in the future is fine by me."

The next pickle I just shoved into my mouth gets stuck in my throat and I start to frantically wheeze and cough. Austin rushes toward me and tries to stroke my freaking back.

"Get away from me," I squeak and bat his hands away. "You're insane."

"Why? Because I finally accept what I want and should have claimed sooner?"

"I repeat, you're insane. I'm not pregnant. You don't have to take responsibility because I feel like shit and most of all, don't feel guilty about stealing my case. Just…don't!"

I rush out of the kitchen and head for the bathroom. Snatching the test from the counter I give it a glance and thank fuck.

"See?" I point it at Austin. "One line. Not pregnant."

He takes it from me and a grin slides over his face along with relief.

"I knew it. Making me an old lady was more out of obligation than wanting me for me." I give a snort and shake my head. "Good thing no one else was around to hear your insanity. Knowing I'm not pregnant you don't have to follow through. Not that I would have accepted your claim anyway. But I can clearly see the relief on your face."

"It is relief because you scared the fuck out of me," the man easily supplies. "But it's okay. You're pregnant so you don't have a choice. You're mine. But you would be mine as well without having my baby in your belly. Like I said; doesn't matter, you're mine."

"What?" I squeak.

Why does this man always make me squeak?

He holds out the test. "The line is faint but it's there. Two lines. Pregnancy. If you don't believe me, use the other test since I bought two. But you need to know it doesn't make a damn difference. Pregnant or not, you're mine. I made up my mind and won't let you walk away."

"Let me walk away? You're the one who left," I growl and snatch the other test out of the paper bag and pull my pants down.

Austin is staring at me and he makes me snap, "Get the hell out of here and let me pee."

"I can watch," he mumbles.

"You did not just say that," I bark.

He shrugs and luckily has the sense to step out

and close the door. Thankful to be able to squeeze out some more pee, I hold the stick in there and the whole waiting game starts again. This time, though? This time I'm going to keep my eye on it and watch the line. Lines. Change. Whatever, I'm going to keep my eye on it.

I feel someone step up behind me and know Austin is standing next to me. This time the test is clearer and it shows two solid lines.

"The other test was a cheap one. I bought both because I didn't know which one was better and didn't want to ask."

I don't know what else to say but, "I'll call the clinic and get another test to make sure."

He pinches my chin and guides my face to face his. "This is a good thing, Jers. Like I said, I made up my mind."

I take my chin from his grip. "I'm glad you think it's a good thing. I've only ever had one relationship. You and I? We don't even have a relationship. We don't even get along most of the time. Hell, my ex cheated on me and died. But getting pregnant from a one-night stand is a good thing? In what world did you grow up?"

"In one where I was the result of a hot encounter that lasted a few minutes. One where my mother kept the pregnancy and me secret. One where my father found out and claimed what was his that very day. And one where they are still together, very fucking happy, and where I am facing the very same thing and am trying to tell my old lady all will be fucking fine because I'm the walking and talking result. Shit doesn't get better than that."

All I can do is stare.

The lamest answer falls from my lips in a whisper. "I don't know if I can be or want to be a mom."

Austin cups my face with both hands. "Sweetheart. I've seen you with Beatrice's kids. You're a damn natural. Even if you've never thought about having kids…isn't life all about unexpected chances and possibilities? Hell, I never expected to feel shit and yet there you are, always in my face and doing things inside my body I can't explain. But that one night together? Everything fell into place. I hated leaving. I texted Archer about meeting you but he told me to stay away. I texted his wife to keep me up to date about you. I contacted you but you never once replied or I would have told you how you drive me crazy."

I can't help but snort. "Drive you crazy? I think it's the other way around."

"See? We have that in common. And just the fact we go head-to-head shows our passion. Let's give us a chance. I know it's going to take a lot to withstand the tests we need to face to be together, but I'm up for anything if I get to hold you every damn night and every damn day."

"Neither side will be thrilled," I muse.

Austin pulls me against his chest. "Archer married my VP's daughter. I'd say he doesn't have a leg to stand on if he starts giving me shit."

"We have to tell my parents before yours. I don't want them finding out from anyone else."

"Agreed," Austin says and places a kiss on the top of my head.

"Okay, you can feed me now, because I'm really

hungry. And I think you're right. It's not mere fatigue or a bug. This pregnancy is kicking my ass and it's barely starting."

I feel his lips brush the top of my head again. "It's not the pregnancy. I'm sure it's been the hell of a few weeks you've had with the move, packing, long drives, stress, one, all, take your pick. But I'm going to make damn sure you're taking good care of yourself from now on."

I step away and glare while I shove the items of the tests into the paper bag and into the trash. "Don't turn into one of those overbearing neandertals."

He leans in and takes my mouth. Pulling back way too fast he murmurs against my lips, "I'm not making any promises I can't keep. I've never had a woman of my own, most definitely not an old lady."

"I'm flattered," I reply dryly.

"You should be." His hot breath feathers over my skin when he places kisses along my jaw. "Being my one and only comes with perks."

A chuckle slips out. "Comes with piercings, you mean?"

His head tips back and the air fills with laughter. He's so enthralling with his rough beard, hard muscles, and tattoos all over his body. It's hard to comprehend he wants to claim me as his old lady. Correction; he *claimed* me as his old lady.

I forgot about his parents but he's right, they too started their relationship with a secret pregnancy because they instantly connected. Due to a lot of things they were kept apart but collided later once more and Pokey, his father, took charge and they ended happily ever after for sure.

I don't know what's in store for us, I guess you never know until you try. But I guess that's what we'll do. And if I get to feel those piercings again very soon, I guess he's right about the perks.

"Come on, I'll add more pickles to your sandwich."

Again, he's right about me being hungry, though the reminder of the piercings releases a craving for something else.

I slide my hands up his chest and wrap my fingers into his leather cut to pull myself to my toes and whisper in his ear, "Mind giving me an orgasm? You kinda owe me."

His low chuckle releases a swirl of tingles to spread through my body. "I do owe you," he murmurs. I reach for the button of my jeans but strong hands bat mine away and before I know it, my jeans and panties are on the floor and I'm feeling the cold tiles against my ass.

Next thing I know his hot, thick, pierced head is nudging my entrance. The tip slides in but he's cupping my face with both hands, staring at me intently while he slowly enters me. This is nothing like the first time and yet it's the same urgency flowing through us.

But the way he's keeping my gaze hostage is where I can see the possessive claim overtaking him with the knowledge he's taking what's his. But most of all, he's telling me without words I belong to him. Pleasure burns through me, pushing away the thought how this moment is far from the reality I ever thought possible and yet this feels so right.

"You're mine. All mine." He times his words

with every thrust and his breathing rapidly turns ragged.

My own breath catches and I can already feel the sweet tingling of my upcoming orgasm. His piercings rub the walls of my pussy while one of his hands slides in between us, rubbing circles over my clit and taking away the ability to think. There's only us. Our groans, our pleasure, our moment where we both commit to one another on all levels.

"Fuck. I'm gonna. Yeah. Come with me, darlin'. Come. That's…fuuuuuuuuck."

He buries his head into the crook of my neck and latches his mouth to my skin. His teeth nip and intensify the pleasure ripping through my body while I can feel his dick twitch deep inside me while he fills my body with hot cum.

My heart is racing and I'm out of breath but it feels so damn good. His lips trace a path along my jaw until he captures his mouth with mine. He might have filled my body with pleasure a mere moment ago but the feelings he taints me with by this tantalizing kiss are mesmerizing.

I let my fingers trail over his bald head, along his jaw, muscled neck, everywhere as long as I can feel every inch of this man. I might have been in a relationship before but this doesn't compare to anything. The connection we have is indescribable and is a mere shadow of what I've encountered.

Nothing, absolutely nothing compares with the way my heart beats within this moment. As if two hearts collided and found a rhythm and share the beat of life itself. And it's thrilling. Scary but at the same time I feel complete.

Austin steps back, allowing his dick to slide out. He pulls off his leather cut and hangs it on the hanger near the door. Stalking to the shower, he turns on the water and helps me out of my shirt and bra.

We take our time to shower and let our hands roam. I'd like to say we're going at it again but our shower time is different than giving into lusty need. There's no rush, no franticness, only slow and sensual.

He wraps me in a large fluffy blanket. Snatching both our phones, he guides me out of the bathroom and up the stairs. The master bedroom is massive and the bed is taking up a lot of space, and so is the TV. Holding up the blankets, I slip underneath and feel the bed dip when he crawls in behind me.

His strong arms pull me against him and he flips on the TV. He shifts and drags me over his chest. With a few clicks he's picked some series to start and even though I slept for hours, I'm content to lie in this man's arms and dream away.

"I still need to feed you," he grumbles.

"Later. I need you more as a pillow right now."

His chuckle flows through his chest and the vibrations make me sigh in contentment. Yeah, we need to prolong this moment for a little bit longer. Reality always comes crashing back way too soon.

"It's such a coincidence you came to gather information about the missing woman's case. I just decided to contact Archer because she still hasn't turned up and I can't find a trace. I think she might not be alive anymore. 'Cause it's highly unlikely she doesn't want to be found by her mother. Her asshole husband I'd understand but–"

"I'm pretty sure she's dead too." I turn and balance myself on his chest to stare down at him. "I asked Archer for a case and he had a file right in front of him. I recognized the hooker we saw getting into the man's car. Archer gave me the case and I explained about your case and how we needed the info."

"Makes perfect sense. Do you have the file with you?"

I shake my head and snuggle back against his chest.

"Fuck. We need to get it. Was there just one dead woman? You guys don't handle a case until it's urgent enough for bodies to pile up."

"Three dead women. All the same MO where they are bound by hands and feet, throat sliced, and someone cut out her tongue and poked their eyes out."

"Sounds like a shitload of repressed anger. If they are bound, the perp has kept them for a few days or what?"

A sigh rips through me. "Yes. The dates between

going missing and found are days apart so he takes his time."

I shift and swing my legs off the bed.

"Where are you going?" Austin grumbles and tries to wrap his arm around my waist to pull me back into bed.

I dash away and waggle my finger. "No way. You're all fifty questions, my head is jumping on the same train of thought so we might as well seize the day and head over to the Broken Deeds MC club-house and get the file out of my room."

"You have a room at the compound?" he growls.

"It's only temporary." I shrug but the way his eyes are narrowing I guess he's not liking it one damn bit.

"We're heading for the clubhouse and your room all right," he says as he gets out of the bed and stalks to a closet to pull out some clothes. "But we're get-ting your things, are talking to your father and call-ing mine and both prez's because you're moving in with me today."

I glance from his naked ass to the massive bed and back to his sculpted cheeks again. I don't find it in me to complain about his demand so I merely nod and feel a dopey grin slide on my face.

Though, I'm not sure how long my bubble of happiness will last with the whole talking to my father part, along with both presidents. But I guess we just have to wait and see. I do wish we could put a pin in it so we're able to dive into the case first.

There are so many questions and leads to track down. And who knows, maybe the husband of the missing woman isn't connected. But maybe he is and we've stumbled onto a killer, one we need to take out.

Life is all about priorities. So, they better react nice and handle it quickly because I have a case to solve. And apparently a doctor's appointment to make. Holy shit. I still can't believe I'm pregnant.

CHAPTER EIGHT

AUSTIN

Having Jersey warming my back on my bike again is a damn good feeling. Knowing she's now my old lady? Fucking perfection. The ride to the Broken Deeds compound is too short to really enjoy it but maybe it also has something to do with not knowing how they will react to my claim.

There are a lot of bikes in the parking lot and when we stalk over to the door, Jersey also remarks, "Crap, seems like everyone is present. I wonder what's going on."

It becomes even more apparent when we step into an empty clubhouse.

"They're in church."

Jersey nods at my words and tugs my hand. "Come on, let's get my stuff. Maybe they'll be finished in a few minutes, if not, we'll come back later. There's no rush, right? But I do think there's urgency in the case we're working on because the last woman was taken a few days before she was found dead. What if he already took another woman?"

We head for her room and she quickly roams around, shoving most of her things into one backpack and a few other things into another bag.

"I have a few boxes with my belongings stored in the garage."

"We'll swing by in my truck to get those," I mutter and glance around the empty room. "That's it? You don't have any other belongings other than two bags and a few boxes?"

I thought women had more shit.

"The boxes are filled with...stuff." Her eyes go down and her cheeks cover with a sheen of redness.

Why the fuck should she be shy, embarrassed?

"What stuff?" I question and try to soften my

voice but it still comes out gruff.

"Stuff I need for the items I design and sell in my online store."

"Why the fuck are you whispering? Shouldn't you be proud about it? If you inherited a fraction of your mother's talent, I'd say you should."

She huffs and when her eyes hit mine she shoots me a glare. "Well, maybe I lost a little confidence because my ex–"

"Your ex was a fucking moron so don't compare anyone with that fucker, certainly not me."

"I make weird dolls. There, happy now?"

The corner of my mouth twitches. "I am. So, did you put that last one you designed in production?"

Her forehead furrows and her face shows confusion.

"A-hole. The sketch in your notebook."

Her cheeks now flush hotter than before. My head tips back and laughter rumbles out. This damn woman makes me laugh more that I have in all my life.

I'm punched against my chest and the words,

"Make fun of me why don't you," are fired at me along with it.

I snatch her wrist to prevent her from spinning around and I give a tug to make her collide with my body, wrapping my arms around her to keep her close.

"I'm not making fun of you. I thought the sketch was awesome. I want one."

"Nice save," she mutters. "Not believable but you get credit points for effort."

"What the fuck? I'm not saying shit 'cause you're my old lady. I'm telling you my opinion. The sketch was pretty damn amazing and I'm happy to hear you're selling them. Better yet, I'd like to hear more because I'm fucking intrigued. And does your old man seem like a person who'd lie to you? To anyone for that matter?"

She releases a choppy breath. "No. You're always brutally honest."

Then it hits me. "That fucker kicked your self-esteem pretty damn hard, didn't he?"

She snuggles tighter against my chest. "He said I

was twisted inside for creating those hideous things. And when I caught him cheating on me, he yelled about how I was the one who drove him to it since I was a rigid cold bitch. One who was beyond mediocre and wouldn't accomplish anything if it wasn't for my tie to those outlaws thinking they're above the law."

"If the fucker wasn't dead, I'd make sure he was roadkill," I grumble.

Silence fills the room until a soft giggle teases my ears. "He did end up as roadkill."

Her head tips back and she's so damn stunning with her caramel eyes swirling with many emotions to make them vibrant and loving.

"So. Fucking. Gorgeous," I whisper and lean in to take her mouth.

Licking the seam of her lips, she opens up and the instant our tongues collide it's as if a surge of pleasure crashes through me. I've never understood the chemical reaction bodies have other than the technicality of it.

But I now understand one can suck up theoretical

information and make the knowledge your own though the experience heightens the value. It's as if my body is on fire, burning for the woman who fucking completes me.

Loud voices make our mouths disconnect. I'd like nothing more than to strip her naked, eat her sweet pussy until she comes on my tongue twice and a third time around my cock, but now is not the time or place.

"Church is done. Time to find my father and Archer."

"You read my mind. Come on, grab your things. You never know, they might be pissed and not give us a chance to gather your stuff before throwing my ass out."

A low growl rumbles through her chest. "They wouldn't. No matter what I'm coming with you. Besides, Archer's wife was Areion Fury MC. Baton–"

"Yeah, we've repeatedly mentioned it back and forth but every situation is different. And it's best not to mention Baton, the issue is still raw and most don't understand why he turned his back on you guys while he was alive all that time. I mean, thinking you're gonna die is one thing but when you survived…no matter what issues or whatever is going on, when you have a family…a brotherhood like you guys have? One doesn't simply walk away. I think there's more to it."

She faintly nods and swings her backpack over her shoulder. "Yeah, you're right."

I grab her other bag and we stroll out of the room, down the hallway and into the main room where all the brothers are coming out of church.

"What the hell?" Jersey gasps underneath her breath.

I follow her line of sight and watch Baton stroll out of church right next to Archer. What the hell in-fucking-deed. The asshole was dead-set to never step foot in the clubhouse again after I found his stupid ass and he had a talk with his club.

Baton sees me and his eyes turn feral. "You," he sneers. "Areion Fury doesn't belong here. Get the fuck out, asshole."

All eyes land on me. Silence is thickening the air

until Wyatt steps forward. Archer holds his arm out, stopping his VP from walking toward me.

"Austin. I don't believe I hired you for an active case. Therefore Baton is right: you don't belong here. And as of a few hours ago our connection with your club is hanging on by a thread. This is the reason I won't hire you again for the foreseeable future. I suggest you leave the premises right now."

What.

The.

Fuck?

"What's going on?" Jersey questions.

"None of your concern: it's club business," Baton snaps.

Archer glares at the fucker and it's a good thing because I'm itching to go for his neck by the way he spoke to my old lady.

"I have an–" I start but Wyatt interrupts me.

"You two, come with me." His voice doesn't leave any room to object and the way his eyes narrow, it's clear he wants a private talk.

I'd like nothing more than to confront Archer for

openly dismissing me but Jersey grabs my fore-arm and tugs. I tear my gaze away from Archer and follow Wyatt out the door. Once we're standing near my bike the man whirls around to face us. I shove both bags into my saddle bags because somehow my gut is telling me we're going to be leaving very damn soon and I'd like to be ready.

"I don't know if you're in fact pregnant or not or what's going on between you two but you gotta put a pin in it."

"What the fuck changed and made your prez kick me out while the asshole has always been the one to drag me into his fucking clubhouse and threw one assignment after the other at me?"

Wyatt releases a heavy sigh. "Baton showed up early this morning. Pissed as hell. He has some story about Makayla being the one preventing him from coming back. How she was the one who suggested for him to heal first and when he was back to the land of the living he owed her and respected her wish to fully rehabilitate first. One week to the next and if you asked me? He ended up falling in love. I guess love has limits since she disappeared on him today leaving a note how it was all a setup. She wanted to hurt Broken Deeds MC. Doesn't make any fucking sense, but there you have it."

"Impossible," I growl. "I know Makayla. She wouldn't do anything to risk bad blood between both MCs."

Wyatt points at my chest. "See? This is why I dragged you out of there. You take her side, Archer takes Baton's side. MC against MC in the damn clubhouse. And I gotta tell you, I'm not buying Baton's story. It's why I'm thinking there's more than a grudge involved and why I mentioned the love angle. His whole demeanor screams as if he's ready to raise hell. There might be truth to his story but some of it might be curved, understand what I'm saying?"

I give a tight nod. "What's the plan? Because this woman right here? She's my old lady and the baby in her belly is mine."

Wyatt rubs a hand over his face. "Fucking hell. Please tell me you weren't about to claim her a minute ago?"

"Okay, then I won't…but I sure as fuck was going to." The corner of my mouth twitches.

Nothing's funny about this situation but I'm not going to back down either; Jersey is mine.

"Then I'm glad you listened and followed me out. I suggest you listen some more when I tell you two to keep it under wraps for now. Give me a few days to dig into the facts of Baton's story and we'll go from there."

I slightly nod. "I can find out on my side what the hell happened. Makayla might be Zack's daughter but she cut ties with her parents and the MC a few years ago. She wanted to distance herself from the club to fully focus on her career. I'm not judging her or anything but the woman is a doctor and ever since she left for med school the woman grew a stick up her ass, if you know what I mean."

"Yeah, maybe that's part of the issue of what's happening. Let's find out more and I'll call you and we'll put our heads together, yeah?"

I hold out my hand for him to shake. "Sounds like a sane plan."

He's about to shake my hand but a voice bellows, "Jersey, get inside. Now."

Our eyes swing toward the clubhouse. Ramrod is standing there with his arms crossed in front of his chest.

"Fuck," Wyatt grunts. "One fucking complication after the other. Maybe it's best she stays here for now."

"Not happening." My eyes slide to Jersey. "You're mine."

She gives me a small smile and her eyes slide to her father. I straddle my bike and fire it up.

She takes a step toward my bike and her father bellows, "Don't do it, Jersey. I forbid you to get on his bike. You have no business with him: we have no business with him."

"I think," Wyatt starts but I cut him off.

"I don't care what the fuck you think. Jersey, your choice, darlin'. If you stay, I'll come back for you anyway. But I'd rather have you with me at all times."

All the words haven't left my mouth yet but my

old lady is already straddling my bike. Curses rush through the air but I mute them by letting my bike roar as we speed out of the parking lot.

We were supposed to go back to my place and go over the case but with everything crashing down on us I set course to head for my club. I'm sure Zack is already aware of some of the shit going on, or he will be soon.

But I do know one thing; no matter what, my president will have my back.

"Are you sure this is a good idea?" Her voice is a mere whisper and I hate she's stuck in the middle of this shitstorm.

I lace my fingers with hers and stroll toward the clubhouse. "There's one huge difference between this clubhouse and the one we just left, darlin'. For one? This is my brotherhood. My brothers have my back no matter what. Secondly? You're not a biker but the daughter of one. The second I voice my claim against my brothers, you will officially be mine and no longer Broken Deeds MC."

She squeezes my hand. "Okay."

I place a kiss against her temple and echo, "Okay."

We step inside the clubhouse and I notice Zack and Dams standing in front of church along with my father and a few of my other brothers. Some of the old ladies are sitting at a table and they smile at my woman while Zack's face turns grim.

"Jersey," my Prez rumbles. "Even if you're working a case with Austin, I think it's best you return home. It's not the right time for a visit. I'm pretty sure after what happened today your father nor Archer would like having one of their own setting foot in the clubhouse of Areion Fury MC."

"Jersey stays," I grunt. "She's my old lady."

Dams' son rubs his hands. "Oh, this is too good to be true."

Dams shoots his kid a glare. The asshole is still green behind the ears and was patched in three weeks ago.

"Austin, Pokey, Dams, church, now," Zack grumbles.

"Prez, I'd like my woman to be present."

Dams shakes his head. "I don't think so."

While Zack says, "Fine," at the same time.

I guide my woman toward church while Dams looks very unhappy. I don't blame the man; his daughter married the president of Broken Deeds MC and now I'm stalking in here with a daughter of one of them while the shit with Baton and our president's daughter just came crashing upon us.

We all take a seat but I'm not waiting on my president to start asking questions. "Mind explaining what happened between Makayla and Baton? Because we just came back from the Broken Deeds clubhouse where I was basically evicted. Archer told me he won't be needing my services again. If it wasn't for Wyatt ushering us out, shit might have escalated."

"Makayla left the fucking country so I can't drag her ass over here and make her explain it to me in person. She's fuck knows where and has no damn cell phone service because no one is able to reach her."

"That sounds fucked-up. Even for Makayla," I mutter, mainly to myself.

"Wyatt told us Makayla left a note how it was all a setup. She wanted to hurt Broken Deeds MC. Does it sound like something she would do? Take care of another biker and tell him to stay hidden and not return? Then all of a sudden leave town with a mere note betraying him and all of you? Not to mention cause damage between two MCs who have been living, and working, next to one another for years?"

Everyone's eyes are on Jersey but no one says anything.

Zack's gaze lands on mine. "She called her twin. In fucking tears. Blabbering about loving someone enough to let them go. Love not being strong on both sides if the other is holding a grudge. Love…fuck. I don't have a clue what drove her to skip town and leave this mess for all of us to solve. Though the anger Archer was spitting at me when he called me a few hours ago doesn't seem like shit is easy to solve this time."

Jersey places a hand on my thigh and I swing my gaze her way. "What is it, darlin'?"

"Remember what Wyatt said about Baton? How

his whole demeanor is as if he's ready to raise hell?"

I slowly nod. "Yeah, the fucker was on edge and was ready to bite my head off for wearing the wrong patch."

"I think that's it. What Zack just mentioned? Loving someone enough to let them go? I think Baton has been eating himself up from the inside out by staying away from Broken Deeds MC. And the way she left, giving him no choice but to return? She… well–"

"Fuck," Dams snaps. "She set him free. Not giving him a choice but forcing him to return to his brothers he misses. Fucking hell, that's screwed up."

"And now the asshole is pissed for being shoved to the side. I know those two mentioned it was just friendship between them but clearly there was more since she confessed to it. Maybe Baton didn't realize it yet and it now flipped to anger. Fucking hell, she did it out of love for that fucker," Pokey adds.

"Basically," Jersey says, a load of sadness tinging her voice.

"We need to take a few days to let it sink in. Everyone is too hyped up. Maybe we can get a hold of her in a few days and talk some sense into her. It's clear she loves him. Hell, she was dead-set to live her own life away from the club only to fall in love with one."

Pokey snorts. "Right, Prez. But the club colors are a little different. In the end it didn't matter, she knew what the brother needed and forced him what the stubborn asshole probably didn't want to do; take the first step into making amends."

"I don't think the note Baton mentions exists. I think there might have been a note but wouldn't have mentioned those exact words. Nonetheless, they caused damage and Baton is taking it out on you guys since Makayla is out of reach."

I give my old lady a smile. "I think you're right."

"All right. Let's give it a rest and get some facts these upcoming days. Now, about you two…how the fuck did that happen?" Zack grunts.

"I've had my eye on her a long time," I confess, making Jersey's shocked gaze land on me. The corner of my mouth twitches. "She's the only one getting in my face all the damn time, and when we were forced to work together on a case we collided beautifully. So much that she's–"

Jersey covers my mouth with her fingers. I slowly shake my head and grab her wrist to free my mouth.

She sighs and mutters underneath her breath, "Fine, let's not tell my parents first."

I feel a surge of pride flowing through my veins when I state the words, "We're pregnant."

My father is the first one out of his chair and heading toward me. He pulls me to my feet and claps me on the back, words of congratulation flowing freely. He switches to Jersey and hugs her close while Dams smacks my shoulder.

Zack is grinning like a loon and shaking my hand. He pulls me to him and slaps my back, giving me the words, "About time, brother. And I can't thank you enough. Those fuckers have taken women from our club, it's about time we steal one of them. Fuck. Gonna be a father, huh? Great, my man. Fucking great."

I grunt a thanks and glance at Jersey. She's wearing a huge smile and it's a good feeling to get some happiness after the shit we just muddled through. Though I know it's fleeting. We still have issues to solve along with a missing persons case that might have shifted to serial killer status.

CHAPTER NINE

JERSEY

"I had a wonderful time, thanks so much for inviting us." I give Orianna, Pokey's old lady, a thankful smile.

She's very sweet and was kind enough to invite us over for dinner. Though, it was Pokey who in fact made dinner. Chicken parmesan and it was amazing. I didn't know what to expect when we walked into the Areion Fury MC clubhouse earlier today, but I was pleasantly surprised.

After talking things through and knowing hints of both sides of the story, it does make some sense. I get the feeling Makayla acted out of love and saw

Baton needed his brothers, though Baton didn't want to face this reality himself. Maybe he didn't deem it possible to return home?

It's going to be tough to get facts on the table and explain them in a rational manner to everyone involved. We also need to contact Makayla because I don't think she has to sacrifice her own life and love to give the other person what he desires. Even more when that person is depriving himself. Shit. We're going to need help to fix all of it.

"Don't mention it." Orianna pats my hand. "I'm thrilled to have you. And I'm even more excited about the little one growing in your belly. My first grandchild."

I glance over my shoulder in the direction of the living room. Austin and his father are watching some football while I'm helping Orianna with the dishes. Knowing she kinda went through the same thing, and all of it basically got thrown into my lap–pun and no pun intended–I decide to open up to her.

"We had sex once and apparently it was enough. Not to mention I woke up to an empty hotel room and the jerk dismissed me not only on a personal level but also professionally. Telling Archer it was me who solved the case we were working on together and yet he was the one handling it." I bite my lip to stop my rambling and wince. "Sorry. We really did collide hard and fast but it ended abruptly. Funny how it was because of the two MC's involvement and today it's yet again the reason why there's trouble."

Orianna chuckles and places her hand on my forearm. "No need to be sorry. And I know exactly what you mean. Pokey and I only had a few minutes in a damn bathroom but it was enough to conceive Austin. And it might be a quicky for some when they hear how our relationship started but for me? It felt like I found the person I wanted to spend the rest of my life with. Due to complications we were driven apart and a lot of stuff happened. Thing is… we found one another and yet here we are, decades have past and we're still together, strong as ever and happy in love."

She glances in the direction of the living room

and back at me. "What I mean to say is, every relationship is different. Only the people wrapped up in it are allowed to have a say what is best and what-not. There are people who date for months before they agree to a solid relationship. Take years before they think about children and plan everything. Still they either end up being happy or divorced. Life is a gamble no matter what precautions you take. And it's when I took a chance and went all in…that's where I found the magic."

"You found magic in a bathroom. At least mine was in a hotel room." I snicker and Orianna giggles.

"Now there's a nice sound," Pokey says as he strolls into the room.

He wraps his arm around his old lady's waist and pulls her close. The look in their eyes when they stare at one another radiates full-on love. It's something similar to what my parents have.

When you're alone you might be one person, and yet you're not complete; it's when you found the right person that you fully become one against everything else. Because that's what these two people reflect. A force strong enough to handle anything.

"Ready to go home?" Austin asks.

"Yeah. We still have some work to do." I take a deep breath and stroll toward him.

"Thanks, you guys. Call if you need anything."

We head out but when we're almost at Austin's bike, his father jogs our way. "Son?"

"Yeah, Dad?"

"Can I have a minute with your woman?"

"I don't think that's a good idea," Austin starts.

I bounce my gaze between both men and I'm intrigued. Austin seems to know why Pokey wants to talk to me but Austin doesn't think it's a good idea?

"What's going on?"

"Don't put this on her, it's my responsibility."

Pokey shakes his head. "No, it's not. You saw what it did with Zack's daughter and Baton. She needs to know."

"Know what?" Instead of asking Pokey I now direct my question at Austin.

He mutters a curse and releases a deep sigh. "Fine. My dad here thinks I'm the key to solving the Makayla issue because I'm the one who bounces between MCs. It's also why he thinks I have a choice after the issue is solved. A choice to switch patches."

"Switch patches? Is that even possible?"

Pokey winces. "Hate to break it down like this but sometimes there are dominant clubs who can forcibly disband a smaller MC. Large MCs most times have rivalries and fight over issues or territory. Broken Deeds is clearly bigger and more dominant than Areion Fury MC. We've willingly accepted supportive roles in the past. If Archer is out for blood, he can certainly try to threaten us to hand over our colors or disband. And in my eyes it's a small step for them to take Austin. Add the part where they have the whole damn government at their back, it gives them loads of possibilities. Austin is a valuable asset. I mean, they have hired his ass many times and I hate to say it." His eyes slide to Austin. "I think it's a better fit. Broken Deeds solves cases, you work cases. It's a no-brainer."

I stare dumbfounded at Pokey. Is he serious?

I grew up in the MC and know a lot about everything but not all technicalities. Most definitely not about one MC absorbing a member of another MC.

I do know Broken Deeds MC is above the law and makes its own rules but seriously? I'm excited to hear this would even be considered an option. Austin always works cases for us already, everyone knows him and he sits in during meetings, it would be logical for him to switch. It would certainly be amazing to stay with my family, but on the other hand, it would mean Austin has to leave the family and MC he was raised in. Talk about a massive dilemma.

"I'm not going to discuss this. I'm Areion Fury MC. Stay out of it, dad, and don't mention anything to Zack or contact Archer either," Austin grumbles.

"Archer has offered you a spot more than once," Pokey fires back.

"And the last time he mentioned he won't offer again and wouldn't accept me either. Hell, he practically kicked me out of the clubhouse."

Shit. This discussion is getting heated and won't go anywhere either.

"Come on." I tug on Austin's sleeve. "Let's go home. We have a case to go over and I'd like to curl up on the couch when we do instead of standing here talking about stuff that isn't going to be solved by the two of you arguing."

"Smart woman." Pokey chuckles. "I knew you'd do good, son."

Austin shoots him a grin and straddles his bike. Sliding on behind him, I wrap my arms around my old man and relish in the way how extremely right this feels. A lot of things might be thrown upside-down in all our lives but this? This right here lets me know we will have the choice to make things right.

When we arrive at his house it also strikes me how he bought his home in a place where it sits right in the middle of the two clubs. His father is right; he really is the key to bringing both clubs back together again.

And I hate to realize the fact he was right to take charge when he recognized the address of Makayla. He will always put the club first and in this case, he put both clubs first by handling it himself.

Does he even realize it himself? Hell, he's been wearing one patch but might as well have inked two because he's an active part in both. A person who claims to be foreign to feelings and emotions has an overload when it comes to a brotherhood.

He grabs my stuff from his saddlebags and we enter his house. I take the bag holding my laptop and the stuff from the case and dig them out to place the items on the table. Glancing through my stuff I now notice I've left my warmer clothes in a box locked away at my parents' house.

"Want some coffee?" Austin questions.

"Yeah. Hey, do you have a hoodie or something? I'm cold and the warmer stuff is in a box at–"

"Loads, upstairs, in my closet. Grab whatever you need." Austin disappears into the kitchen and I make a quick run upstairs.

Once in the bedroom I now notice the dog bed in the far corner near the bed. Sadness hits me. The way Austin always keeps things clean and has very limited stuff in his house, he still has his dog's bed in the bedroom while she died a few weeks ago.

Again, the man has an overload of feelings and emotions. It's just bottled up with a different label. He really is a magnificent man, not a boring one for sure. I grab the first black hoodie I see and shrug it on.

From the corner of my eye, I catch a glimpse in the mirror of my back and it makes me smile. The Areion Fury patch is staring back at me and it's kinda ironic for a Broken Deeds MC girl. Pokey's words slide through my head again and it makes perfect sense. These two MCs have been braided alongside one another for decades.

Austin is sitting at the table, going through the file about the three dead women I laid out for him. Placing the documents and photographs in three different piles, he takes out his little notebook and looks up when he hears me coming.

A sly smile spreads his face. "Good choice, darlin'."

I roll my eyes. "Smooth. Real smooth."

He holds up a photograph. "This is the one that caught your eye when you saw the case. You're right. The tattoo, the hair. Again, you were right, it wasn't her natural hair color. The wig was found at the scene, though."

"Like taking out the trash," I murmur and notice a bag of chocolate candy.

I reach for it but Austin snatches the bag and pulls it toward him. "Mine."

"I'm yours too, therefore you need to share," I simply state and lean over the table to grab the bag for a second time.

He still won't let me have the bag but throws one my way.

"Really?" I growl. "How generous."

"Put the wrapper in the bowl." He points at a bowl where two wrappers are already sitting in.

I demonstratively unwrap the candy, pop it into my mouth, and shove the wrapper into the pocket of the hoodie.

A dreadful sigh rips from his throat. "It's my hoodie. In the past I've seen you shove just about anything in your pocket and even use it as a tempo-rary trashcan. I better not find any when you return *my* hoodie."

"I've confiscated the hoodie. It's mine now." Dismissing him, I take his notebook and try to make sense of his writing but seriously, "My doctor's handwriting is readable compared to this."

He snatches it from my hand. "I use a code. It's my notebook, no business for anyone else."

"Gotta learn how to share," I mutter.

"Drink your decaf coffee," he shoots back.

I wrinkle my nose and wrap my hands around the mug. He throws me two other pieces of candy as he starts to talk while glancing through the few papers he hasn't placed on a pile yet.

"Three women. All of them have the same markings. Bound wrists, sliced necks, eyes are poked out, tongues missing. They weren't raped. Strange. There's also no DNA or signs of a struggle."

"Some missed patches of hair, did you get to that part yet?" I question.

"As if someone has repeatedly grabbed them by their hair."

"And dragged them across the room because they

all have lacerations on their knees," I finish for him.

His eyes find mine. "Have you done any research yet?"

"No. I've only glanced through the file when it landed on my lap. Wyatt and I headed straight over to you because I wanted to have all the info on the dude to crosscheck before I fully dove into the case."

"Good. See if you can find any security cameras on the corners where he might have picked up the other two. If we assume it's the same guy. I mean, he could have dropped the woman off after a blow job in the car and then the killer was her next client."

I place my empty mug on the table and reach for my laptop to fire it up, snatching another piece of candy and shoving the wrapper in my other pocket. Austin glares at me and points at the bowl. Ignoring him, I click on the software I need to see if we can get a glimpse of the two other missing women on camera on the night they went missing.

"He had a white car, right?" I question.

There's a murmur and I glance over the laptop

to see him furiously chewing. He gives me a slight grin and this time repeats his words clearer. "White Volvo. S90."

"I didn't know you had a sweet tooth," I muse and find a garage who has security cams for the cars in its parking lot and it actually gives a glimpse of the street corner where one of the women was last seen by her friends.

"Ever since I had a taste of your pussy," he fires back and I have to stop fast-forwarding the footage to make my gaze collide with his.

"Work," I grumble and drag my eyes back to the screen.

Dammit, my whole body tingles with the reminder of his tongue doing magical things while we need to focus on catching a killer. Good thing we have a small window of time to check since the woman's friend gave a time range when she got into a car.

It doesn't take long for me to find it and when I zoom in I can tell it's definitely a white car. Turning the laptop, I show the footage to Austin and he agrees it's a white Volvo fitting the car owned by

Nils Grift.

"We can make it out because we know what we're looking for," Austin says and grabs a paper from the pile on his left. "Cops searched most of the footage but not the one from this camera."

"Cops searched a minimum radius for the best footage. This is not enough for a conviction while we don't need it to catch a killer."

"Yeah." Austin releases a sigh. "It's the one angle I can't complain about when it comes to cases Archer throws my way. You guys can work fast without limitations. I have to go through a lot of hoops to get shit done. And the cases I've consulted on with the cops I've also hit limitations where Broken Deeds doesn't have any."

"Great perks," I muse and notice something when I see the white car drive off. "Austin, come look at this."

He rounds the table and it gives me the time I need to rewind. I feel him at my back when I replay the moment.

"Sonofabitch. There's someone in the backseat."

"Yeah, I thought so. The shadow is faint but if you're thinking the same thing?"

"We have to give thought to the fact we might have two perpetrators," Austin finishes for me.

"Not much to go on. It could be clothes hanging in the back or items stuffed onto the backseat? Okay, I'm going to leave this for now. Did you run a full check on Nils? His wife? Anything you like to share?"

Austin places a kiss on the top of my head. "Go wild, darlin'. Dig through everything you can find and we'll compare notes. I know from previous assignments you work best with a clean slate. Let your brain run your own path. More coffee?"

"Thanks," I mutter and I'm already letting my fingers dance over the keys.

First, I'm going to comb through Nils' background. Work, life, financials, social media, anything I can get my hands on. Then it's time to check out his wife, Rose. Running the same checks, I also find two shared accounts.

"Did you know he was married before Rose? His

wife died, cause of death was inconclusive."

"You're shitting me."

"Nope, records were sealed due to the woman being the daughter of a diplomat. But that doesn't make sense. I'm going to make a note to look into it but I also have to check out the cabin Nils bought three days before his wife went missing and two days after the first woman went missing."

"He bought a cabin? How? I checked his financials."

"It was a joint account." I turn my laptop and show him a split screen.

One side shows the money transfer, the other is the ownership papers with Nils' signature along with the date on it.

"Fuck me, you're good."

I shoot him a grin and am about to say, "I know," but my attention is drawn to my phone which I've just turned back on. I had about twenty unread messages and a load of missed calls. I didn't know what to say to anyone from my family so I turned it off when we went into the Areion Fury MC clubhouse earlier today.

"You should answer them or at least send a message you're okay."

"I know." My chest squeezes. "I just don't know what to say or who I should send the text to. I'm not ready to call and talk to either my mom or my dad. He ordered me to come to him like a dog, Austin. I just...I don't know."

"Text Beatrice. She's the president's old lady. You don't have to explain anything or tell her everything. You know she will keep it to herself or prepare Archer for the inevitable." Austin places my phone near my hand.

"You're right." I sigh and tap the screen. "Might as well go all in," I mutter to myself and type out a long message starting with the words, "I'm going to need your advice," and ending with, "I'm pregnant and accepted Austin's claim to become his old lady." Everything in the middle is wrapped with Areion Fury and Broken Deeds MC along with Wyatt in the mix as well if she wants to share this information with someone to talk it through.

My phone stays awfully quiet the whole night. Austin and I work through all the information we've gathered on the case we're working on until the both of us can't keep our eyes open and head for bed. Wrapped in each other's arms, we end up talking some more about personal stuff.

I fall asleep hoping tomorrow will be a day filled with chances and solutions, because we surely can use a break. Not just on a business level either. But I guess for all of us personal is entwined with business. *Club business.*

CHAPTER TEN

AUSTIN

Waking up with body heat covering my chest is an overwhelming feeling but one I embrace. After working together with this woman till deep into the night, we moved to the bedroom to get some sleep but ended up talking for a few more hours.

We've known one another all our lives, our background, family, shared memories of barbeques and all other shit both MCs arranged, yet on a personal level there are still things left unspoken. There are many things I find intriguing about my woman and her working drive is one.

She's brilliant when it comes to computer work

but hearing about her business selling and designing unique dolls is enthralling. There's an intimate passion, one she can pour all her devotion in and get so much in return than a solid income.

One I had to do a doubletake from since I didn't know people spend that much money on dolls. But they are unique and she even has a limited edition series clients are willing to do just about anything to get their hands on the next one.

And the way her eyes lit up when she was talking about it? Fuck. Such open passion, it's easy to get sucked into her enthusiasm. Fucking annoying to know that asshole ex of hers put her down and basically made her think she wasn't right in the head.

Good thing the blockage she put in place to protect herself is gone; I showed her to be damn proud of her accomplishments and how awesome her creations are. At least, that's what I think. And the way her eyes were radiating warmth I'd say she accepted my words.

We have a full day ahead of us. First, we're going to stake out the cabin that is in Nils' name. Another amazing quality in my woman; a sharp brain. Thinking in solutions and ways to get there. How she gathered information in this case is amazing and we now have several leads to check out.

But that's for later. For now, I'm staying right where I am because I'm allowed to revel in her warmth. The way I handled things on our first case together made me think I blew every shot to hell to have her as mine. Yet it was the very moment that bound us together.

Fuck. I still can't believe she's pregnant. Another welcome addition to my life; expanding to the fullest. I've been alone for many years and it's something you really don't think about when life is passing you by.

And to have this woman in my arms is like standing rooted to the ground, taking in the scenery and realizing life is fucking breathtaking when you have everything you need to take one breath after the other.

Her weight shifts on top of me, hands lingering and it rips a groan from me when her fingertips slide downwards. I don't know if she's wide awake or dreaming but if she keeps this up she's going to be the star of my wet dream.

"Fuck. Yes," I grunt when she finds my dick and wraps her tiny hand around it.

I groan and let my eyes fall shut. The day barely begun but it's starting out as a slice of heaven thrown at me. And when I feel her body shift, lips placing a trail of kisses downward? Heaven just crash landed on earth and made me the center witness.

No way am I keeping my eyes closed. Getting on my elbows I watch how my woman has made a place between my legs and has her gaze settled on my hard, pierced cock. Enthrallment and lust openly swirling in those caramel eyes.

"I have been wondering," she murmurs, and I'm not sure if she's even talking to me or to herself. "What it would be like to see up close, feel up close, taste…up…close."

My breath freezes in my lungs when her tongue sneaks out and licks my pierced slit, fucking flicking it before her lips surround the tip and I watch how inch my inch disappears into her hot mouth.

"Motherfuuuuuuckkkk. Woman," I grunt and slide my fingers into her hair, fisting it to keep her in place because the way she takes my cock? Fuck. I don't ever want it back; she can have it as long as she keeps sucking.

Her head is bobbing and my hips shoot off the mattress to demand more. Her hands are at the root of my cock, an automatic stop to make sure I'm not choking her. Good thing because the way her magic mouth works me over? I'm bound to lose all my intelligence and ravish her mouth like a madman, not caring if I give her death by cum either.

That's how far gone I am. She starts to hum, vibrations shooting through my dick while her devilish tongue teases my piercings, the underside of the thick head, I have no clue what the hell she's doing as long as she keeps going.

A tingle starts low in my spine, shooting through my balls and before I can warn her, I'm releasing a flood of cum down her throat. I can feel her swallow, taking everything I got while I let my eyes feast on her face that's washed with the same pleasure wave I'm riding.

Everything with this woman is fucking captivating. My whole body is lit with emotion and it feels like I'm hotwired with so much energy, I can take on the whole damn world as long as she's by my side.

Taking her breathtaking face into my hands, she lets my cock fall from her lips and it's a damn sexy sight branded into my memory for a lifetime. I pull her up and kiss the fuck out of her, not caring at all if I'm tasting myself.

I roll us over and tell her, "Gotta return the favor. Give you pleasure while I get my fill of your delicious pussy."

Her eyes once more burn hot and she gasps when I find one of her nipples, catching it between my teeth while I knead her other magnificent breast in my hand. I'm about to switch breasts but the damn doorbell starts to ring.

I ignore the damn thing and work my way down but right when I'm about to get my mouth on her pussy? Both our cell phones start to ring while the doorbell screams for our attention as well.

"Fucking hell," I grumble.

Jersey chuckles and mutters, "You can say that again." As she jumps off the bed and grabs her phone.

I do the same and see it's Wyatt calling me while at the same time Jersey states, "That's weird, it's Beatrice."

"Wyatt," I grunt into my phone while I hear Jersey answer hers.

"Open the door, sleeping beauty, this is your wakeup call," Wyatt chuckles.

"What the hell?" I mutter.

"Beatrice and Wyatt are at the door. Hang up and get dressed. I told Beatrice we'll be right there."

The both of us jump into our clothes and since I'm good with just my jeans and leather cut, I'm the first one jogging down to answer the door. Letting the both of them inside, I head for the kitchen without looking back. They follow me into the kitchen where Jersey joins us. Beatrice gives Jersey a hug and I can hear her murmur a congratulations at the same time Wyatt smacks my back.

"I heard you officially claimed her?" he asks.

I grab a few mugs and merely nod. Within a few minutes I'm handing out coffee and we're moving into the living room to sit at the table that's still littered with all the documents of the case Jersey and I are working on.

Both of these two are Broken Deeds MC so there is no breach of privacy or delicate information. If any other person would be inside our house we would have put everything away.

"What brings you two here?" Jersey boldly asks and I'm happy she's the one cutting straight to the point.

Beatrice shoots my woman a smile. "I wanted to check up on you and since your text yesterday mentioned Wyatt was aware of your situation, he wanted to tag along. Also, Baton seemed off to the both of us. He's angry. After church he practically raided the bar and locked himself in a room at the clubhouse. Something doesn't add up and Wyatt wanted to know if you heard any news from your side about the whole Makayla and Baton situation."

Jersey looks at me and I give her a nod. She's the one who has a theory, one I assume is very likely.

"They can't reach Makayla. She left. As in fled the country to give Baton no other choice but to return home to you guys. I'm pretty sure she loves him. So much in fact that she gave him up because she saw what not going back did to him. He has a whole load of pride. Everyone who knows him is aware of this little fact. Hell, the whole wanting to live forever fuels this statement as well. And it's so sad. But you have to realize, Zack and Blue are devastated. They want to reach her and ask what the hell is going on as well. But what Baton mentioned? A setup? No…I don't think that's the truth. Did she leave him? For damn sure. But there's more to the story and I'm thinking Baton knows it damn well but doesn't want to face the truth."

Wyatt and Beatrice both nod thoughtfully at Jersey's words.

"Zack says it might be wise to let it settle for a few days while they try to find a way to contact Makayla. Meanwhile we have a case to work on.

I know Archer told me he wasn't hiring me anymore and kicked me out, but that doesn't mean I'll simply hand over something my company is also involved in. Besides, it's a massive red-flag case and while I'm assisting Jersey, we need some form of backup." I direct my attention at Wyatt. "You were her backup on this one, right?"

Wyatt grunts.

"We managed to tie two of the three dead women to Nils Grift. One Austin and I witnessed the connection and the other I found through a security cam of a garage. The angle wasn't perfect but you can make out the type of car owned by Nils."

"And there might be another person involved," I add to Jersey's statement.

"Two perps?" Beatrice questions.

"Yeah. There was a figure in the backseat. Like I mentioned, the angle of the camera wasn't perfect."

"Any other progress or lead? You mentioned backup, what's your next move?" Wyatt directs his question to Jersey.

"Nils has a cabin. We were going to head up

there to check it out. He might be using it to drive the hookers there, do his thing and dump the bodies afterwards."

Wyatt rubs his chin and processes Jersey's words. "Sounds too simple, a fucking cliché if you ask me. But we can't let it pass. Okay, I'm coming with you guys."

"Me too," Beatrice announces.

Wyatt shakes his head. "I don't think that's a good idea."

"Oh, shut it. I'm not a helpless chick. I know how to throw a punch, been in shootouts, and all that other stuff you guys do on a regular basis. You know I don't scare easily. Besides, the kids are with Archer's parents and I have the day off."

"This is so not a good idea," Wyatt grumbles. "But you know what they say, the fun starts when all things go to shit."

"They don't say that," Jersey scolds and starts to pile up the documents and shoves them into a file.

I take it from her and lock it away in a drawer. "Okay, I have to get dressed and then we'll leave."

Within a few minutes we're all in Wyatt's SUV, the women in the back, Wyatt is driving while I'm in the front seat going through my messages. My prez texted to keep me updated about Makayla. Apparently, she left the country with a friend of hers who is also in the same line of work.

I text the info to Jersey to keep it between us and maybe the both of us can find out more about the friend and track her down since Makayla obviously knows how to dodge a trace. I get a smiley face in return.

The silence in the car is broken when Wyatt starts to ask a few questions about Nils. We get him up to speed about the other details of the missing person case and it doesn't take long for us to get near the cabin.

Wyatt parks the SUV in a large parking lot. The cabins around here are surrounding the lake and though every cabin has their own parking space, most use the parking lot. It's for this reason there are over twenty cars here.

"See how I mentioned the whole cliché thing?

It wouldn't be smart to abduct a woman, bring her here to drag her off into a cabin in the woods," Wyatt point out.

"Cabin at the lake," Beatrice clarifies.

"We saw these women willingly get into his car, remember?" Jersey easily supplies. "They get money in return for sex and I'm sure that's what he tells them so they go willingly. No dragging off into a cabin kicking and screaming so who would notice? Keep an open mind, anything is possible."

"Stockbroker gone serial killer. Yeah, anything is possible," Wyatt mutters and double checks his gun while I do the same.

"I should carry one," Beatrice quips.

"Fuck, no," Wyatt snaps. "Prez would have my balls if he knew I brought you along. Weapon you up? He'd have my dick along with it and maybe shove it up my ass for good measure."

Beatrice snorts. "Pussy."

Wyatt glares while Jersey chuckles. "Play nice kids or I'm going to rat you out to Big Hoss."

Now the both of them are glaring at my woman

while I'm the one chuckling and pulling her close to place a kiss on the top of her head.

I clear my throat. "Okay, you guys. We might appear to be two friendly couples who are doing a little sightseeing together, but we need to focus."

Wyatt falls in step beside me while Jersey and Beatrice follow us. We have to walk for a mile or two before Nils' cabin comes into sight. The white Volvo is parked outside. I'm sneaking glances inside the cabin while the others do the same as we walk straight past it.

The lake comes into view and it gives us the chance to fake enjoy our surroundings and talk over our first impression. With our eyes still on the place it's not hard to pick up on the fact there's a man stalking around inside the cabin.

"Since his car is in front of the cabin, I'd say Nils is there," Jersey starts.

"True," Wyatt says. "The glimpse I caught through the side window told me as much."

"Checking out the cabin is…oh, wait. Oh, there's an opportunity," Jersey mutters and points at the lake to make it seem we're all glancing at the stunning scenery.

This because there's a man stalking out of the cabin and into the Volvo. We all watch how it drives off.

"We're going in, right?" Beatrice grins and rubs her hands. "Don't mind me, I'm stuck behind a computer more often than not and I honestly prefer it that way, but being out in this awesome scenery really spices things up."

Wyatt groans. "Why don't you two keep an eye out while Austin and I double check if the cabin is indeed empty before we go inside?"

Both look like they're about to object but we're already strolling toward the cabin. Both women instantly stake out their surroundings, making it possible for us to get close to the cabin.

One glance through the window shows the inside of the main room. There's a bed with a woman strapped onto it. I glance at Wyatt who is staring at the same scene in front of us. His eyes narrow and I know what he's thinking.

"We can't leave her. I'm guessing we're jumping into action?" I whisper.

Wyatt nods and grabs his phone. "I'm texting Archer so he knows to send a few teams our way. We need this cabin handled and hunt down that fucking white Volvo. It's pretty clear Nils is the killer."

"We have to be careful, though. There could be someone else working with him, remember?" I fire back.

He lifts his chin and works fast; the back door isn't much of a challenge for Wyatt. The man has skills with breaking and entering and I follow him into the cabin within minutes. It's quiet inside and we enter through the tiny kitchen.

Wyatt is palming his gun, as am I. The living room isn't very big and the first thing both of us notice is the way the woman is bound and gagged, lying on a filthy bed. The bed has dark stains, resembling old and dried blood. The woman has similar features to Rose, the woman who's missing.

"I'd say it's safe to say Jersey was right about her hunch with the two cases being connected," Wyatt says.

I'm about to check on the woman but Beatrice comes rushing into the cabin hissing low, "He's coming back!"

"Fuck," Wyatt and I growl in sync.

I glance through the front window and notice the Volvo heading for the cabin.

"Where's Jersey?" I whisper hiss.

"Outside keeping an eye on the front," Beatrice whispers.

"Stay in the kitchen and out of sight, backup is coming but we're taking this fucker right now," Wyatt orders Beatrice.

My nerves flare not having eyes on Jersey.

"I have a bad fucking feeling about this," I grumble.

"One walked out, one is walking back in as we speak. There's two of us," Wyatt snaps underneath his breath.

We both take aim and wait for the door to open. Nils steps inside at the same time Wyatt growls, "Hands where we can see 'em, Nils Grift."

There's a gasp coming from behind him and I now know for certain the woman bound to the bed isn't Rose because she's right behind Nils.

"Yes, please arrest him. He's held me captive all this time. He's a killer. Please help me," Rose begs.

"You're full of shit," Jersey states from behind her.

And that's when all goes to hell right in front of my eyes.

CHAPTER ELEVEN

JERSEY

I watch how Nils steps inside the cabin, silently following him is Rose who is right behind him and freaking smacked her husband around when they got out of the car just now. So weird to see the woman not missing but in fact very much alive and in full control of the man I've seen pick up hookers. It's not making any sense but my gut is screaming at me how Rose is not innocent.

"Hands where we can see 'em, Nils Grift," Wyatt growls from inside the cabin.

Rose gasps and start to ramble in an overly pleading tone, "Yes, please arrest him. He's held me captive all this time. He's a killer. Please help me."

"You're full of shit," I blurt and the woman whirls around, eyes bulging and it's as if she instantly knows she has nothing to lose.

I could curse myself for letting my mouth ramble before thinking because the woman has a knife in her hand before I can blink. Fucking hell, I've trained for this and it takes one second to stall for this woman to jump me by surprise and have a knife at my throat.

"Where the hell did you pull the knife from? Between your breasts? Bad move, Rose. Bad. Move. Better hand it over if you want to live because my old man is going to eat you alive. He has murder written all over his face right now, can't you see?"

"Shut up," the bitch screams in my ear.

"Hey," Wyatt snaps. "Eyes here, Rose. No one is going to freak out, hear me? And I do have to agree, Jers."

I shoot Wyatt a glare and feel the blade pressing into my skin. Wyatt is holding Nils at gunpoint and

I'm sure Austin has his eyes on me but I can't look his way. I failed him. Hell, I failed myself by not defending myself and letting this woman get the better of me.

"Let her go. Right fucking now," Austin bellows in a deadly tone.

"No. I'm calling the shots here. Nils, get their guns. Come on you no-good sonofabitch." Her hand doesn't tremble and there's no hesitation when she nicks my skin. "And don't think I won't cut her throat. I will."

I can feel warmth sliding down my neck. My heart is beating in my throat.

"You're not getting my gun, asshole," Wyatt snarls and in one smooth move his palm shoots out and connects with Nils' nose, knocking him backwards and he crumbles to the floor.

Panic surges through me. I noticed Beatrice earlier in the kitchen but I'm not seeing her now. Did she rush out? Call for backup? My eyes land on Austin. My only rock within havoc. One breath fills my lungs as our eyes connect and his gaze goes over my shoulder, head slightly jerking to the right.

The only opening I have where I'm not blocked by her arm. I hope he's right and I understand him correctly. I jerk from her grip but at the same time I feel the knife break through my skin and a hard shove in my back, causing me to roughly stumble forward.

I can't catch myself and the table in front of me hits my stomach. Falling back on my ass I push the pain to the background and scramble up to glance behind me. *I have to see her coming this time.*

Except Rose has fallen to her knees, the knife is on the floor and she's holding onto her head. Beatrice is standing behind her with a big rock. Clearly, she went out the back and rushed around the cabin to knock Rose over the head.

Rose starts to swear. "Goddammit, you should hit him. I'm only defending myself. Who are you people anyway? The whole 'hands where I can see them' says cop but neither of you showed your ID or wear a uniform. Did that asshole not only cheat on me with hookers? Let me guess, he stole most of my money so his gambling also got him into trouble with the mob. That's it right?" Her gaze swings toward Nils. "You're such a worthless piece of shit. I should have ratted you out the first time you murdered a woman. Now they're going to kill us both."

"Outside," I croak and my hand goes to my throat. "You said…you…I don't know what happened the first time but you're the one pulling all the strings. She ordered him to pick up a new hooker. How they're going to end this one because, and I quote 'she's not doing it for me anymore, I'm bored.'"

I pull my hand back from my neck and it comes back crimson. "That's not good," I mutter.

"Fuck," Austin grumbles and is standing in front of me.

One arm is occupied with the gun still aimed at Rose but his attention is fixed on me.

"Bee, can you see if there's a clean cloth or something around here? We need to stop the bleeding," Austin orders. "Jers, look at me. It's going to be okay, you hear me?"

"What the hell does that mean?" I wonder out

loud and glance down at myself.

"Oh, that can't be good," I mutter and see the front of my shirt is now drenched with blood. Pain in my stomach flares up. "I don't feel–"

My knees buckle and I half catch myself on the table I bumped into earlier, slowly sinking to the ground.

"I'm going to sit for a bit," I tell myself and suddenly remember the bandana I shoved into the pocket of my hoodie earlier.

I start to press it against my neck and see movement from in front of me. Rose lunges for the knife. A gunshot roars through the air and the woman crumbles down to the floor. The bullet impacted between the eyes.

"Nice reflexes," I compliment my old man. "Better than mine. I should have seen the knife coming. I'm so stupid."

A flair of nausea hits me and I'm starting to feel faint.

"Shut the hell up. Your reflexes are fine. Anyone can get a jump on someone at some point in life, we've all lived through it. And you're going to live through it too. You hear me? Stay with me dammit."

"EMTs are a few minutes out, Archer will be here soon," Wyatt says and he seems so far away.

My hand slowly slides down.

Austin curses. "Beatrice, take my gun and aim it at that fucker on the ground. We're not taking any other risks. Dammit. This is a grand fuckup."

"If I had a gun earlier–" Beatrice mutters.

"Stop fucking around," Wyatt snaps. "Bullshit about 'what if' always happens after the fact and is only going to cloud your brain. Austin, stop the bleeding, Beatrice, cover. Focus on your damn jobs."

"Thanks VP," Austin mutters and it makes me smile.

"He's not your VP but that did sound nice coming from you," I remark, and I'm not sure why I said it.

"I think so too, Jersey girl," Wyatt chuckles. "Maybe I'm going to find a way for him to officially call me that. But you gotta hang in there to see it happen."

I give a snort and slowly blink. "I'm tired."

"You've lost a lot of blood," Austin mutters. "I can't put too much pressure on the cut or it'll make breathing difficult. Dammit."

"Ah, dilemmas of life. Maybe it's a metaphor for you. You know, choosing between MCs," I muse.

"Could you save your breath for survival?" Austin pleads, and the fear in his eyes is killing me.

Well, it's more like he's watched someone slowly kill me and I'm dying in his arms. Shit. Am I dying? Panic starts to kick in and I have to distract myself. I blurt the question roaming around in my head while it's just us in here and Wyatt being the VP and making a joke earlier must know.

"Wyatt, can Austin switch chapters?"

Wyatt's face appears in my vision. "Austin can do anything he wants, Jers."

Faintly I see my father's face coming into view. Am I dreaming? I must be. He wasn't here. My brain becomes fuzzy and it's becoming harder to stay awake. And eventually I fail to think and slowly sink into darkness.

– AUSTIN –

"Stay with me. Dammit she passed out, where are those fucking EMTs," I roar.

"Oh, fuck," Ramrod grunts and is suddenly standing beside me. "Move, let me hold my daughter."

"You'll have to pry her from my cold dead fingers because I need to make sure my old lady lives before I so much as leave her side," I bite out my words but keep my focus on my woman. "Wyatt, come on man. Are they here yet?"

"She's not your old lady," Ramrod snaps.

"Keep it together," Archer growls. "Ramrod, your daughter has two sides, leave Austin be and walk around. Besides, EMTs are here, step back, both of you."

EMTs surround me and I'm having a hard damn time handing my woman over. Her body is slack and she looks so fucking pale.

"She's pregnant," I croak. "She hit the table. Fuck."

I get to my feet and hold both hands to my head

while I stare down. They're dealing with the bleeding. The cut on her neck was fairly deep on one side. Fucking lucky the bitch didn't nick an artery. Jersey did lose a lot of blood though. And if she hit the table hard in her belly, she could have internal bleeding. And the pregnancy. Fucking hell.

"Keep it together, Austin," Archer snaps and his face comes into view. "I can't have you going on a rampage and the look on your face tells me you're ready to kill each and everyone in this room."

"She's my old lady," I whisper in a tone so faint and filled with emotion, I don't even recognize my own voice. "I can't lose her. She's…I can't. She's my life, man. She's light. She makes me fucking function like the blood in my veins." Desperation starts to fill me. "If I lose her I wouldn't be able to fucking function. I'd be nothing."

I grab Archer's cut and bellow, "I can't keep it together because she could be dying right fucking now while all she has to do is live and I can't control it."

Archer is shoved away from my grip and I'm staring into brown eyes similar to Jersey's but missing the caramel.

"We're not going to let her die. You hear me, son? She's tough. I've taught her to be tough. Open your ears, you hear that? Her heartbeat might be faint but it's there so you heed Prez's words and keep it to-fucking-gether, hear me?"

I swallow hard and give Jersey's father a tight nod.

"Good. Now when our girl is taken care of, you and I are going to have a long fucking talk. And I hope to fuck I misheard the pregnant part because I'm too young and too good-looking to become a grandpa."

"You're going to become one either way," I state with determination and keep my eye on Jersey who is now transferred onto a stretcher. "If not now then very soon in the near future."

Ramrod shakes his head. "Like I said, long talk, asshole. Fuck. But I guess if anyone mixes with our DNA, you're a great catch with the high intelligence and all." He grabs my cut and pushes me to start walking. "Only one thing wrong with you."

"What's that?" I ask as we walk out the door behind the EMTs who are taking Jersey into the ambulance.

"Since you grabbed your head with your bloody, slick fingers, those have the right color. Your patch, though? Not so much." He slaps my back. "But it's easy to fix. Come on, you're in the ambulance. Keep an eye on Jers. Archer and I will meet you at the hospital.

– JERSEY –

I'm disorientated but the first thing coming into view is Austin's concerned face.

"Hey," I croak.

There's a straw placed at my lips and when I turn slightly, I see my mother. "Here, take a few sips."

The water soothes my dry throat. My father–who is standing right next to my mom–squeezes my ankle through the blanket and gives me a smile. "You gave your old man a bit of a scare there. But I wasn't worried. You kick ass. I knew you'd pull through."

"Whatever, man," Austin grumbles. "I saw your eyes water."

"That was your blurry vision, nothing to do with me," my father growls.

"Men," my mother sighs. "You're okay now, that's what matters."

I shift and try to sit up. "I'm sticking with a desk job, though. I might not like working with computers but the whole knife slicing, bullets flying, things up close and personal isn't my thing."

My stomach hurts and my hand goes to it, the memory assaulting me how I knocked into the table.

I swing my head toward Austin and don't have the nerve to ask. I was shocked to find out I was pregnant but to lose something when I haven't been able to fully process or so much as plan or schedule an appointment with the gynecologist is breaking my heart.

"The place of impact wasn't anywhere near the uterus. It's too early in the pregnancy for a sonogram but the exams they performed show the pregnancy is still intact. Two more weeks or so and then we get a sonogram to hear the heartbeat."

The emotional look he gives me along with his words rips a sob from my lips. His hand reaches out and he gently wipes away the tears sliding down my cheek.

"Everything is okay, darlin'. I promise." He leans in and places a kiss on my lips.

I swallow hard and face my parents. "You're not mad?"

A flash of surprise slides over their faces.

"Why should we be mad? Sweetheart, getting hurt in the line of fire is something each and every one of us have experienced at one point. And if you don't want to go into the field and work from behind your computer instead, that's fine too," my father quickly rattles out his words.

My mother smacks his chest. "She means our future son-in-law."

"Oh." My father shoots me a grin. "Archer has been trying to get him to wear a Broken Deeds MC cut for quite some time now. And don't worry about the issues between the two MCs at the moment. Archer and Zack have been in the waiting room together with their old ladies and there hasn't been any blood spilled yet. I'd say you two did a nice job in getting them together."

Another smack lands on my father's chest, making him grunt.

"Don't like you getting hurt. Especially almost getting your head sliced off. Horrible, horrible situation. Nothing to do with that being the reason to bring those two presidents together," my father quickly adds.

My mother takes my hand and gently squeezes. "We're happy for you, sweetie. As long as you're happy, we'll be ecstatic. Especially when you throw in a baby. But you need to take it slow for a bit. You've lost quite a bit of blood but both Austin and your father would like to take you home."

"The doc will be back shortly to check your vitals. Then we'll know if you're okay to come home." Austin clears his throat and adds with a little more determination, "Our home."

"It's a good thing you live close," my father mutters underneath his breath while he glares at Austin.

I already feel a bit better with a hint of bickering and chitchat. And it also triggers awareness of the reason why I landed in here.

"Rose is dead. You shot her. I saw it happen, right?" I question, needing to be sure.

"Yeah," Austin grunts. "You were right. Nils has been rattling Wyatt's head off about every single detail. Seems like Rose caught him fucking a hooker in their own bedroom. Nils was so shocked to see his wife walking in. He wanted to step away but apparently Rose didn't accidentally catch him because she walked in with a huge kitchen knife. She ordered him to keep pressing the woman's head into the pillow. He suffocated her. Nils blames Rose but it was his actions that killed that woman. The whole slashing their throats, cutting tongues, and poking eyes out was Rose's way of getting out her anger while she made Nils watch."

"And Rose has been keeping him under her thumb the whole time," I finish for him.

"Right. She's the one who bought the cabin under his name. Nils said he thought she was setting him up to take the fall for all the murders but Wyatt said the fucker got off on it too. Apparently Vachs and Benedict found a load of videos when they searched the cabin and his laptop. Their sexual activities weren't healthy from there on out, let's just stick to that, shall we?" Austin cringes.

My father leans in. "More like nutjobs who made snuff films. But the whole why and how doesn't matter. We might not understand their fucked-up reasons anyway. End of the line either way. Rose is dead and Nils is going to jail for a very long time."

"Case closed," Austin grunts.

"Case closed," I muse.

A deep breath slides out of me and I give my old man a smile. "Can you get the doctor or a nurse? I feel so much better and I would like to go home. I'd rather sleep in our bed."

"I'll go," my mother says.

"I'll help," my dad offers and shoots me a wink.

The door closes and Austin is hovering over me. "Finally, I have you to myself."

I reach out and cup the side of his worried face.

"I'm okay," I tell him, feeling the need to let him know to stop worrying.

"You fucking scared me," he whispers with a load of emotion. "Don't try to slip through my fingers like that again. I love you, woman. So damn much I don't care if the world crumbles around us: as long as I have you beside me."

I let my thumb slide over his cheek. "I love you too."

I can barely get the words out before his mouth covers mine in a soft and tender kiss, as if he needs to seal the deal, molding a promise of love we just put in place. My lips tingle, my belly flutters, and my heart warms, knowing our lives will be shared as one from here on out.

CHAPTER TWELVE

Six weeks later

AUSTIN

All I can do is stare. It looks like something from a horror movie. A gray mass with black and white… hell, I don't even know how to describe it and I know exactly what it is but it's…it's…fuck. I'm a daddy of a tiny fetus. Heart beating strong and it's fucking perfect without being able to count fingers and toes.

Before this woman I would have never deemed it possible to have this kind of chemistry flowing inside my body and now? I fucking thrive on it. My fingers hover over the sonogram picture we added to the refrigerator door and I feel a smile slide in place.

Whenever I get something out of the refrigerator,

hell, every time I walk into the kitchen, I give the picture a glance. A few months from now he or she will be in my arms and I can't wait.

I bring the bottle of water with me into the living room and place it in front of Jersey. She's been working on a new case. Something about debt collectors. Two deaths are tied to one man and yet there is no solid evidence.

She mindlessly nods and opens the bottle, taking a few sips before letting her fingers fly over the keyboard. I grab my own notebook and take a seat across from her. Archer put me on another case.

Over the past few weeks there hasn't been much time to talk technicalities. It wasn't such a surprise to see him standing on our doorstep three days after Jersey got out of the hospital. He walked inside my house like nothing happened and rattled about a case he needed my help with.

I might still be wearing an Areion Fury MC patch, but Archer made it clear I'm also Broken Deeds MC. He would like nothing more than for me to fully become a part of their MC. And to be honest? I might as well.

It would sure make things easier and will also lift the burden of handling my own business and the administrative part of it. And I really do like taking Broken Deeds cases more than my own through my company with all the limitations.

But for now, the club has gone through enough with Baton leaving like he did. Again. At least this time they all know he's not dead, but he won't be coming back either. Fucked-up, especially for his parents and his twin, though their relationship was kinda rocky already with his own faked death incident.

Zack and Archer shared their thoughts when Jersey was in the hospital. And with a little help of Broken Deeds MC they tracked down Makayla within two days. She answered some of Beatrice's questions and it was exactly how we thought the situation with her and Baton was.

Makayla saved him that day, pulled him out of the ocean and got him the help he needed. She also gave him the time to heal and the months of rehabilitation needed for his arm. She knew who he was; Broken Deeds MC. He knew she was Areion Fury MC. They decided it was best for him to stay hidden.

Wrong decision, but there you have it. Makayla saw how he missed his brothers, more when I confronted them. And those two lived together for months, growing a solid friendship. But for either one it became more but those idiots never voiced said feelings.

Makayla saw how missing his family and brotherhood was slowly killing him inside and forced Baton to return to his brothers by leaving. She did leave a note but it didn't say she did it to get back at Broken Deeds MC. The whole anger part was all Baton who hated himself more for not being honest about his feelings toward Makayla. Talk about a royal fuckup.

I'm glad I only had to endure the cliff notes version of it when Beatrice came by to explain all of it to Jersey. I guess it's a sappy love story where Baton got a kick in the balls and it activated some brain cells, enough for him to get on a plane and go to his girl.

He gave up his leather cut completely and with full awareness and an open heart he chose his woman. But with it they both left their family behind for good seeing they moved to Africa to open up a clinic. It's still a sensitive issue with every brother of Broken Deeds MC, though deep down they respect his wishes to pick his woman over the club.

Here I am thinking about accepting Archer's request, but it would feel like betraying my brothers. Though, Zack and all the others have told me many times they support my choice and seeing both clubs have been entwined for decades, it won't be such a shockwave in comparison to the Baton issue.

I glance over my notebook at my woman. Her hair up on the top of her head, bundled together. From over here it seems like she shoved a pencil in there too. Yeah, pretty sure there is. Her caramel eyes are fixed on the computer screen and I not only love this woman but I also respect the fuck out of her how she balances not one but two jobs.

She's my old lady, she carries our baby in her belly and I want nothing more than to call her my wife and ink my skin with her name. Decision made. I place my notebook on the table in front of me.

"Jersey," I grunt and lean forward on my forearms.

"Hmmm," she hums and skims her eyes over to me and back to her computer screen.

"We're going to get married and we're going to call Archer to get an appointment to get our patches inked."

Her eyes stay on her screen for a few breaths before they crash into mine. Blinking a few times, she starts to sputter, "What? Wha…you. I…come again?"

"Married. Property patch, you and I," I repeat.

"Are you saying?" she croaks.

"I am saying," I repeat and stand to stalk around the table.

She meets me halfway and jumps into my open arms.

"Yes," she squeals and hugs me tight.

"Do you think Lynn is busy? Maybe she can come over and ink me tonight, otherwise Vachs or Hayley. Hell, maybe even Archer himself. We're going to wait with yours until the baby is here, though."

She starts to sputter again and untangles from me.

"For real?" she huffs. "Ugh. You can't be serious."

"I am. There's a tiny risk of infection and statistics say–"

Her fingers are pressed against my lips, silencing me so she can give me the words, "Fine, fine. Whatever. We'll wait with mine. Now, where are you going to put yours?"

Her voice turns to liquid sex and I'm ready to strip naked and let her tongue do a little sight searching on my body to let her pick a spot.

I wrap my fingers around her wrist and pull her hand away, leaning close to place a kiss on the corner of her mouth before I tell her, "I saved a special spot on the side of my neck."

She leans her head to the side and glances at the

spot I just mentioned. I'm basically inked all over and I've been meaning to get something inked there but for some reason I never did. Now I know why because it's damn perfect. I grab her hips and with ease I hoist her up and gently place her over my shoulder, careful not to put pressure on her belly.

She squeals and I smack her ass as I head up the stairs. "Enough work for now. I'm going to give some special attention to some of my favorite spots of your body to see where my property patch will be inked."

A giggle flows through the air and I slowly slide her down my body. She's wearing one of my hoodies again and I can only imagine all the stuff she shoved into her pocket. The corner of my mouth twitches.

She's already stripping her clothes and I'm shedding mine while my eyes feast on her exposed body. I take one step forward. That's all it takes for my hands to palm her ass and drag her against my body. My hard length is caged between us.

I gently lay her down on the mattress and pull back to get my fill. Lush, mouthwatering curves;

my woman has a slamming body. I grab both wrists and place them above her head.

"Keep them there," I rumble and my eyes are already locked on my next target because by this move?

My woman curls her back and pushes those amazing tits toward my mouth. With my hands free, I let a finger trail over her breastbone and curl it around one breast. Her nipples are already hard peaks, begging for my attention.

Unable to resist I let my tongue trail over her pretty pink areola and catch her nipple with my teeth while my fingers tease the other. She's so damn responsive when it comes to her breasts. I'm pretty sure her pussy is already wet and willing but I want her begging underneath me before I slide myself deep.

I kiss her breast and huskily tell her, "I was thinking this is a nice spot." Kissing the side of her other breast I add, "Or here."

I trail down to her sweet pussy and rub my beard over her skin.

"Maybe here, only for me to enjoy."

"Please," Jersey whimpers.

"Yeah." I slide a bit up and place a hand on her side. "Maybe here?"

"Ink the damn thing all over my body like wallpaper for all I care just eat my damn pussy, Austin," she growls.

A bark of laughter rips from my throat but when she starts to growl, huff, and glare I instantly lean forward and dive into the mouthwatering feast before me. Flattening my tongue, I slide through her folds and let her taste enter my mouth. Her hands fly to my head to press me closer and I pull back.

"Hands above your head." I nip the inside of her leg and she squeals but instantly obliges.

I keep our gaze locked when I lean forward and tease her clit with the tip of my tongue. I love her boldness to hold my stare. It allows me to see her face wash with pleasure with every flick and suck.

"Austin, please." The soft plea falls from her lips and the sexy as fuck gasp is my undoing.

I grip her ass and bury my face against her pussy,

sucking the orgasm from her body and letting her fall into a load of bliss. My name is now hitting my ears as a reward and I'm about ready to blow a nut myself.

Shoving my own need to come to the back of my mind, I focus solely on letting my woman flow until she's ready to come down from the orgasm cloud she's riding. She sags back into the mattress and that's my cue to surge up and palm my cock.

I place the fat head at her entrance and let her wetness pull me right in. Wanting to go deeper, I straddle one leg and hook the other one over my arm to create a different angle. Leaning forward I'm able to slide deeper and I inch closer to her face.

Her hot breath flows over my lips. Our gaze is heated, connected, crackling with fire as our bodies move in sync. This right here is what it's all about. Fueling your body with the kind of energy that will last a lifetime.

The feeling is overwhelming and when her pussy starts to clench, I'm ready to surrender. And I guess I'm always ready when it comes to her. She splinters apart underneath me and it triggers my own pleasure.

Consumed. A moment in life where there is no hitting a pause button, and yet this is as close as you can come. Bliss. Body filling with ecstasy while glancing down at my woman who is experiencing the same high.

I'm trying to catch my breath and it's a strain but I have to give her the words, "I love you," and place my forehead against hers.

Her hands circle my body and she pulls me close. "As I love you."

Words are the cherry on top while our bodies almost ate the whole damn cake. But it's something one can never get their fill of because life with the right woman is fucking sweet. And I don't know where this shit is coming from. My brain must be fried from coming so damn hard with her taste coating my tongue.

And if it tastes this good? Life will only get sweeter from here on out.

EPILOGUE

Nine years later

JERSEY

"Statistics say," I hear Gemma, our oldest daughter, start and glance in her direction to see her getting into the face of Halton, Zack's eleven-year-old grandson.

"They say," Halton cuts her off. "Girls who blabber about statistics are killed by people who get annoyed. Nobody likes a know-it-all."

I suck in a sharp breath and am about to stalk over but our eight-year-old puts her tiny fists on her hips, raises herself on her toes and presses her nose against his to growl, "Not this girl, because I know more than a hundred and thirty-seven ways to kill you and about seven good ways to dispose of a body without anyone ever finding said body."

Halton rears his head back and I feel a grin spreading my face to see how much she just put this boy in his place by throwing statistics back at him; the very reason their head-to-head started.

"My grandma brought brownies. Want to come with me to see if we can steal a few before the barbeque starts?" Halton asks–steering their discussion into another direction–and clearly surprising Gemma, and me along with it.

Gemma's face washes with confusion. "Why did your mood change? I don't understand."

My heart squeezes how our daughter is so very smart and way advanced for her age–inheriting the photographic memory genes from her father's side– but is missing some of the interaction and people skills due to the fact she really is a little know-it-all and skipped playing with toys and headed straight into cracking codes and sucking up advanced assignments school provides for her to keep her brain occupied.

But I always love seeing how she seeks her own strength by confronting and being fearless in speaking her mind.

I'm glad to see Halton is grinning at Gemma and shrugs. "The details you just mentioned are things I appreciate and am curious about. You know my dad is the president of Areion Fury MC, right? I'm going to be a president one day. I'm not into all those boring statistic stuff. Maybe we can be friends and I can call you when we're older and you can tell me."

Now it's Gemma who shrugs and simply says, "Okay," apparently his explanation soothed her brain.

They both stroll toward the clubhouse and I can actually breathe a little better. Scary, though. Every stage of raising kids is hard and every child is unique. Gemma is an outspoken girl and luckily both Pokey and Austin have experience with a photographic memory and it helps to guide her.

Karter, our five-year-old son, is luckily still running around with dinosaurs in his backpack and is more interested in the kickboxing lessons Blue teaches to the kids of both MCs than sucking up information. We're all lucky to have so many friends surrounding us.

Not just one MC but both. Due to this there are three generations entwined and when I glance over the large backyard of Areion Fury MC, it's easily to notice the long-lasting friendship appearing in every generation. Though, it does make me cringe to see my own daughter staring up at the future president of Areion Fury MC while he's grinning down at her.

"What's that face for?" Austin chuckles and follows my line of sight. "Is that Halton with Gemma?"

"Yep." I release a deep sigh and add, "She's way advanced. I'm not ready for teenager stuff. Not to mention, letting my mind slide to the possibility of our daughter getting hitched. Especially not to a potential president. Did I mention another MC? Wow. I think this is why they keep having these barbeques and frequent family gatherings, don't you think? It's the older generation's fault. Maybe we should go. You snatch Gemma and I'll grab Karter, I think I saw him chasing your father who was trying to hide behind a tree because that man never gets too old to play hide and seek." I turn toward the man who is still the love of my life and spikes my heart with a mere wink of his eye. "You know, sometimes it makes me question his high intelligence."

Austin wraps an arm around my waist and pulls me close. "It's exactly why he plays hide and seek. The man spends his whole life playing stupid to hide his intelligence in plain sight. It's brilliant."

"You never hid yours," I mutter and snuggle closer.

"True. But it also made me stand out. I think you're the only one who got in my face about it. And if I remember correctly…you were about Gemma's age when you started to repeatedly ignore my personal space."

His words cause me to wince again. Most definitely not something I want to think about because I was intrigued by him at a young age and as a teenager it spiraled into a major crush.

"We're skipping all cozy get-togethers from now on," I firmly state.

His laughter rumbles through his chest. "Come on, let's take Dane for a walk. They won't fire up the grill for another hour at least."

Austin gives a sharp whistle and our rescue dog, Dane, jolts up, grabs his ball, and trots toward us. He's a Dutch shepherd we decided to adopt two months after we got together. I remember very vividly the empty dog bed Austin still had in his bedroom and office when we got together. This while he tossed out all of Sophia's bowls, toys, and leashes.

I actually thought it was endearing how he kept Sophia alive by honoring her name onto his skin. But I know she was also his buddy in the years they spent together. Like we now have Dane. A workout partner, one who joins him when he goes for a run and who stays with me when Austin is out on a job.

Dane was two years old when we adopted him and he might be eleven years old now, but he still chases a ball as if he's a puppy with a whole lifetime of energy inside him. I link our arms and give one last glance in our daughter's direction, knowing both our kids will be watched by everyone here in the backyard of Areion Fury MC.

Austin leans down and grabs the ball from Dane and throws it into the large field. Dane rushes after it and it allows me to get a glimpse of the warm afternoon sun shining bright in a blue sky. It's absolutely gorgeous and I love the serenity of it.

The warmth and beauty is stunning yet simple and it allows me to take a deep breath and be thankful for the simple things in life. My gaze slides down and it lands on Austin who is looking at me intently.

A smile tugs his lips. "Now there's a better look on you than the wincing and worry I saw earlier."

"There will always be wincing and worry." I pat his chest and lean down to scoop up the ball Dane threw at my feet. "But it's good to have someone pulling you out of everyday thoughts and slide your attention into another direction, making you see simplicity."

"Simplicity," Austin muses.

"Uh huh. The sun, its warmth, gorgeous blue sky and the pleasure of a dog running after his ball. Simplicity. Small enjoyments that don't cost a thing.

You. Your smile. A simple hug. Concerns about our children growing up too fast and a world around them wanting to take a bite at every turn."

"Not so much simplicity…your thoughts lean more toward balancing life. You know–"

I quickly press my fingers against his lips to halt his words. "No way are you going to throw 'Statistics say,' at me. No wonder our girl starts most of her sentences with that exact line."

His head tips back and laughter rips out. This beautiful, muscular, inked man shakes his head and glances down at me with a load of emotion.

"Statistics are obtained by a study of data, it helps, gives needed insight. Our girl is smart. And luckily, she has you…a mother who sees simplicity and knows when to place fingers against lips to shut people up. But most of all? We all make it work; together. Growing one day after another into our skin, brain, relationship, into the air to reach the damn sun…because our kids are getting big fast. But they're doing all right, don't you think?"

My mind slips back to how Gemma handled

herself and not only stood up for herself but also wasn't afraid to ask questions for clarity. Austin is right, life is about growing. It's close to a decade ago when we were first thrown together by Austin and started working together. And we've grown immensely since then.

"We're doing all right," I muse and lean against his chest.

His arms surround me. "More than all right."

Dane barks and we both laugh and break apart. Austin grabs the ball and throws it into the field again.

"Baton and Makayla made it," he remarks.

"I heard. Haven't seen them yet but Blue told me they brought their two boys with them this time."

"They've gotten so damn big and I couldn't tell them apart. Damn twins. Two drops of water, like Baton and Benedict were at that age." Austin shoots me a smile.

"I'm glad they're back to visit," I tell my husband and he pulls me close again, placing a kiss on the top of my head.

Baton and Makayla haven't had an easy life after they moved, and it took years to repair the damage of broken trust and ripped emotions to mend between MCs and those two. But it's all in the past now. And luckily we're at a point in time where an arranged barbeque is a moment where families are united and the difference of a patch on a cut doesn't matter.

Though when my eyes hit the skin on Austin's neck where my name is inked with the patch of Broken Deeds MC, I can't help but smile with pride. I have the very same patch with his name inked on my collarbone. Both Broken Deeds MC and yet we're standing on Areion Fury MC property.

His family background is one, I am the other, and yet in the end…it's one solid brotherhood, standing strong. And we wouldn't have it any other way.

I smile when I see Dane plunk down at our feet, tongue all out and panting like crazy. Austin's fingers slide underneath my chin and he tips my head back to give me a toe-curling kiss. I dig my fingers into the leather of his cut and pull him close to let myself drift away while the warmth of the sun shines down upon us.

Austin groans and pulls back, placing his forehead against mine. "It's going to be a long day if I have to walk around with a damn hard on until we're ready to go home. I don't think you're up for some fun against a tree, right?"

I glance around and point out the obvious, "No trees."

"Fun in the grass then," he grumbles.

I cup the side of his face and smile as bright as my heart. "I'm always up for some fun, no matter the time or place. As long as it's with you."

I'm hoisted up in the air with my next breath and squeal when he takes the both of us to the ground. He rolls us into the long grass until he's hovering above me.

His eyes are flaming hot when he says, "Remember that when you find pieces of grass in your hair and everywhere else. Maybe even a grasshopper or two."

He doesn't give me time to respond and holds my lips hostage with his. Tongue swirling against mine and making my belly tingle with anticipation. Wait…did he say grasshopper?

Austin chuckles against my lips and pulls back to peer down on me. "It was the grasshopper comment, huh?"

"The mention of insects crawling everywhere isn't very appealing, no." I shove against his chest and the man rolls us, making me straddle him.

His hand sneaks down in between us and he starts to unzip. "How about minimum exposure, maximum pleasure?"

"Smart man." I give him a beaming smile and gasp when he easily pulls my underwear to the side, allowing him the room he needs to slide inside me.

"Your man," he rumbles and grabs my hips. "Fuck, you feel good. It's the same cheesy line sliding through my head every damn time I get to bury myself inside you. Fucking heaven."

My head tips up and I glance at the bright blue sky, knowing his words hold truth; *Fucking heaven.* Right here or any time and place for that matter; as long as the one who holds your heart is right there with you.

THANK YOU

Thank you for reading Jersey and Austin's story. Gaining exposure as an independent author relies mostly on word-of-mouth, so if you have the time and inclination, please consider leaving a short review wherever you can. Even a short message on social media would be greatly appreciated.

If you would like to read all the stories of the first generation of Broken Deeds MC along with two other, standalone second generation stories?

Here's the link to all the books:

books2read.com/rl/BrokenDeedsMC

SPECIAL THANKS

My beta team;
Neringa, Tracy, Tammi, Lynne,
my pimp team, and to you, as my reader…

Thanks so much!
You guys rock!

Contact:

I love hearing from my readers.

Email:

authoresthereschmidt@gmail.com

Or contact my PA **Christi Durbin** for any questions you might have. facebook.com/CMDurbin

Signup for Esther's newsletter:

esthereschmidt.nl/newsletter

Visit Esther E. Schmidt online:

Website:
www.esthereschmidt.nl

Facebook - AuthorEstherESchmidt
Twitter - @esthereschmidt
Instagram - @esthereschmidt
Pinterest - @esthereschmidt

Signup for Esther's newsletter:
esthereschmidt.nl/newsletter

Join Esther's fan group on Facebook:
www.facebook.com/groups/estherselite

MORE BOOKS

LOST VALKYRIES

MC

UNRULY DEFENDERS MC

UNRULY PROTECTOR

COWBOY

BIKERS MC

Swamp heads
SERIES